Jo

Placing her hands on her hips she added, "And I'd appreciate it if you would keep from underfoot."

"Underfoot?" Bas growled. In the blink of an eye, he'd crossed the room and backed her against the far wall in the cramped office. "You wouldn't know underfoot if it bit you, Jocelyn. *This* is underfoot," he said heatedly, pressing his body intimately to hers.

"Don't push me," he warned huskily. "Especially not for all the wrong reasons."

Jocelyn frowned, refusing to back down. "With you there couldn't be any *right* reasons. And if you didn't understand, then let me make it crystal clear. You're not the boss of me."

His eyes met hers and he gazed into their angry depths. He was experienced enough to see beyond the anger and to notice something else, something she was trying like hell to fight—deep longing, need and heated desire....

BRENDA JACKSON

is a die-"heart" romantic who married her childhood sweetheart and still proudly wears the "going steady" ring he gave her when she was fifteen. Because she's always believed in the power of love, Brenda's stories always have happy endings. A *USA TODAY* bestselling author of over forty romance titles, Brenda divides her time between family, writing and working in management at a major insurance company.

In her real-life love story, Brenda and her husband of thirty-four years live in Jacksonville, Florida and have two sons. You may write Brenda at P.O Box 28267, Jacksonville, FL 32226, e-mail her at WriterBJackson@aol.com, or visit her Web site at www.brendajackson.net.

nightHEAT
BRENDA JACKSON

KIMANI
ROMANCE

To Gerald Jackson, Sr., the man who
showed me what true love was all about.

To all my readers who continue to enjoy my love stories.

To my Heavenly Father who gave me the gift to write.

And God called the light Day, and the darkness He called
Night. And the evening and the morning was the first day.
Genesis 1:5 KJV

 KIMANI PRESS™

ISBN-13: 978-1-58314-778-8
ISBN-10:   1-58314-778-0

NIGHT HEAT

Copyright © 2006 by Brenda Streater Jackson

www.kimanipress.com

Printed in U.S.A.

Dear Reader,

When I first penned my Madaris series I knew those books would be connected by family ties and friendships. The same held true with the Westmorelands and now with the Steeles. Whenever you pick up one of my novels I want to introduce you to new friends, as well as give you the chance to visit with old favorites.

You met Sebastian Steele in *Solid Soul*, and from the time he made an appearance in Chance and Kylie's story, I knew he would be the hero of the second book in the FORGED OF STEELE series. I also knew that it would take an extraordinary woman—like Jocelyn Mason—to show a workaholic like Bas that all work and no play results in plenty of lonely nights. What Bas needed was a lesson in how to have fun and Jocelyn was quick to oblige.

Join Bas and Jocelyn as they bring on the night heat and discover how much fun falling in love can be!

Enjoy,

Brenda Jackson

Prologue

"What do you mean I need to take time off work for medical reasons?" Sebastian Steele asked, squirming uncomfortably under Dr. Joe Nelson's intense gaze. It was that time of year again—the company physical. An event he detested.

Last year Dr. Nelson—who to Sebastian's way of thinking should be staring retirement real close in the face—had told Sebastian that his blood pressure was too high and as a result he needed to adopt a healthier lifestyle, a lifestyle that included improving his eating habits, taking the medication he'd been prescribed, becoming more physically active and eliminating stress by reducing his hours at work.

Sebastian had done none of those things.

It wasn't that he hadn't taken the doctor seriously; it was just that he hadn't had the time to make the changes the man had requested. Sebastian, better known as Bas, was single and used to grabbing something to eat on the run. Asking him to give up fried chicken was simply un-American. As far as taking the medication the doctor had prescribed, well, he would take the damn things if he could remember to have the prescription filled.

Then there was this thing about becoming physically active. He guessed having sex on a regular basis didn't count. And even if it did, that would be a moot point now, since he'd broken his engagement to Cassandra Tisdale eight months ago and hadn't had another bed partner since.

Last but not least was this nonsense about eliminating stress by cutting his work hours. Now that was really asking a lot. He lived to work and he worked to live. The term *workaholic* could definitely be used to describe him. The Steele Corporation was more than just a company to Sebastian; it was a lifeline. He thoroughly enjoyed his job in the family business as troubleshooter and problem solver.

"You heard me correctly, Bas. I recommend that you take a three-month medical leave of absence."

Sebastian shook his head. "You can't be serious."

"I'm as serious as a heart attack, which is what you're going to have if you don't make immediate changes."

The muscle in Sebastian's jaw twitched and his teeth began clenching. "Aren't you getting a little carried away about this? I'm thirty-five, not seventy-five."

"And at the rate you're going you won't make it to forty-five," Dr. Nelson said flatly.

Sebastian stood on his feet, no longer able to sit for this conversation. "Fine, I'll take a week off."

"One week isn't good enough. You need at least three months away from here." Dr. Nelson leaned back in his chair and continued his speech. "I know you don't want to accept what I'm telling you, and of course you're free to get a second opinion, but my recommendation will stand. And I will take it to the board if I have to. If you don't make some major and immediate changes to your lifestyle then you're a stroke or a heart attack just waiting to happen. I'm going to make sure you get to live to the ripe old age of seventy, like me," Dr. Nelson ended, chuckling.

Bas rolled his eyes heavenward. "What if I take two weeks off?" he asked, deciding to try and work a deal.

"You need at least three months."

"What about a month, Doc? I promise to give KFC a break and lay off the fried chicken, and I promise—"

"Three months, Bas. You actually need at least six but I'm willing to settle for three. At the end of that time you'll thank me."

Bas snorted before walking out the door. He seriously doubted it.

"Your brothers are here to see you, Mr. Steele."

Bas frowned, wondering what they wanted. Just as he'd known they would, they had bought into Dr. Nelson's recommendation as though it had been the gospel according to St. John. He was thankful his brothers had given him a week to tie up loose ends around the office instead of the two days Dr. Nelson had suggested.

He stood, crossing his arms over his chest, when the three walked in. There was Chance, who at thirty-seven was the oldest Steele brother and CEO of the corporation. Then came Morgan who was thirty-three and the head of the Research and Development Department. Donovan, at thirty, was in charge of Product Administration. Of the three, Chance was the only one married.

"I take it that you're still not excited about taking time off?" Chance said, dipping his hands in his pockets and leaning against the closed door. "But even I knew you were becoming a workaholic, Bas. You need a life."

Bas glared. "When did you become an expert in my needs?"

"Calm down, Bas," Morgan said, sensing a heated argument brewing between his two older brothers. "Chance is right and you know it. You've been spending too much time here. Time away from this place is what you need."

"And I'm backing them up," Donovan said, crossing his arms over his own chest. "Hell, I wish someone would give me three months away from here. I'd haul ass in a second and not look back. Just think of the things you can do in three months, all the women you can—"

"I'm sure he has more productive things planned," Chance interrupted Donovan. Bas figured his eldest brother knew just where Donovan was about to go. But Chance's other assumption was dead wrong. Bas didn't have anything planned. Before he could voice that thought, there was a knock at the door.

"Sorry to interrupt, Mr. Steele, but this just arrived by way of a courier and it looks important," his secretary said.

Bas took the envelope she handed to him and frowned, noting the return address. An attorney in Newton Grove, Tennessee. Seeing the name of the city suddenly brought back memories of a summer he would never forget, and of the man who had turned the life of a troubled young man completely around.

He ripped into the letter and began reading. "Damn."

"Bas, what is it? What's wrong?"

Bas glanced up and met his brothers' worried, yet curious expressions. "Jim Mason has died."

Although his brothers had never met Jim, they recalled the name. They also knew what impact Jim Mason had had on Bas. While he was growing up, Bas's reputation for getting into trouble was legendary and he dropped out of college, deciding to go off and see the world. Sebastian had met Jim when he'd been around twenty-one. In fact, the older man had gotten Bas out of a tight jam when Bas had stopped at a tavern in some small Georgia town for a cold beer and ended up getting into a fight with a few roughnecks. Jim, who'd been passing through the same town after taking his two daughters to their aunt in Florida for the summer, had stopped the fight and had also saved Bas from going to jail after the owner of the tavern accused him of having started the brawl.

Jim had offered to pay for any damages and then advised Bas he could pay him back by working for his construction company over the summer. Having been raised to settle all his debts, Bas had agreed and had ended up in the small town of Newton Grove.

That summer Jim had taught Bas more than how to handle a hammer and nails. He'd taught him about self-respect, discipline and responsibility. Bas had returned home to Charlotte at the end of the summer a different person, ready to go back to college and work with his brothers alongside their father and uncle at the Steele Corporation.

"How did he die?"

"Who's the letter from?"

"What else does it say?"

Bas sighed. His brothers' questions were coming to him all at once. "Jim died of pancreatic cancer. The letter is from his attorney and it says that Jim left me part of his company."

"The construction company?"

"Yes. I have a fourth and his younger daughter has a fourth. His older daughter gets half."

Bas had never met Jim's two daughters, Jocelyn and Leah, since they had been in Florida visiting an aunt all that summer, but he knew that the man had loved his girls tremendously and that they had held Jim's life together after his wife had died.

Bas quickly read a note that was included in the attorney's letter. Afterwards, he met his brothers' curious stare and said warily, "Jim wrote me a note."

"What does he want you to do?" Chance asked.

"He was concerned that his older daughter, Jocelyn, would have a hard time managing the construction company by herself, but would be too proud to ask for help. He wants me to step in for a while and make sure things continue to run smoothly and be there for her if she runs into a bind or anything."

"That's a lot to ask of you, isn't it?" Donovan asked quietly.

Bas shook his head. "Not when I think about what Jim did for me that summer."

For a long moment the room was quiet and then Morgan said, "Talk about perfect timing. At least now you know what you'll be doing for the next three months."

Bas met the gazes of his three brothers. "Yes, it most certainly looks that way, doesn't it?"

Chapter 1

"And there's absolutely nothing that can be done to overturn Dad's request, Jason?"

Jason Kilgore wiped the sweat from his brow. Over the years his office had survived many things. There'd been that fist fight between a couple who'd been married less than five minutes, and that throwing match between two land owners who couldn't agree on the location of the boundary lines that separated their properties.

But nothing, Jason quickly concluded, would remotely compare if Jocelyn Mason took a mind to show how mad she was. Oh, she was pretty upset;

there was no doubt about it. She had already worn a path in his carpet and the toe of her booted foot seemed to give the bottom of his wingback chair an unconscious kick each time she passed it.

"There isn't anything you can do other than to offer to buy out your sister and Mr. Steele," he finally said. "Have you spoken to Leah about it?"

"No."

Jason knew that in itself said it all. Jocelyn and Leah had always been as different as night and day. Jocelyn, at twenty-seven, was the oldest by four years and had always been considered a caregiver, someone who was quick to place everyone else's needs before her own. She also believed in taking time out and having fun, which was why her name always came up to spearhead different committees around town.

Responsible Jocelyn eventually became the son Jim Mason never had, although he had tried to balance that fact by sending her each summer to visit an aunt in Florida whose job was to train her how to comport herself like a lady. Jason had seen her dressed to the nines in satin and sequins at several social functions in town, and then on occasion, he would run into her in Home Depot wearing jeans and a flannel shirt with a construction work belt around her waist. Jocelyn had managed to play both roles—

lady and builder—while working alongside her father in the family business, Mason Construction Company.

Then there was Leah.

Jason readily remembered Leah as being one rebellious teenager. After her mother had died when she'd turned thirteen, Leah had become a handful and had given Jim plenty of sleepless nights. She had hated living in Newton Grove and as soon as she turned eighteen, she couldn't wait to leave home and abandon what she perceived as a dominating father, an overprotective and bossy older sister, and a boyfriend who evidently had been too country to suit her taste. Her return visits over the years had been short and as infrequent as possible. But she had come for the funeral and it was a surprise to everyone that she hadn't left town yet.

"Do you know of Leah's plans? Do you think she's going to stay?"

Jocelyn shrugged her shoulders. "Who knows? She's welcome to stay as long as she wants. This is her home, too, although she's never liked it here. You know that. But Leah is the least of my worries now since I believe I can buy her out. What I want to know is why Dad thought this Sebastian Steele deserved a fourth of the company."

It was Jason's turn to shrug. "I told you what your

father said to me, Jocelyn. One summer this guy
Steele worked for him. They became close, and
leaving him a part of the company was a way to let
Steele know how much your father thought of him."

Jocelyn turned with fire in her eyes, placed her
hands palm down on Jason's desk and stared at him.
"Why this Steele guy and not Reese? If anyone
deserved a part of the company it's Reese," she said,
speaking up for her father's foreman.

Jason blew out a breath. Jocelyn had finally gone
into a rant, and was definitely in fighting mode now.
"He did leave Reese Singleton a substantial amount
in his will," Jason reminded her.

"Yes, but it wasn't part of the company."

"Jim had his reasons. He thought a lot of Reese
and hoped the money he left him would set him up
in his own business."

Jocelyn knew her father's reasoning. Although
twenty-six-year-old Reese had worked as the
foreman for Mason Construction for years, everyone in town knew of Reese's gift with his hands. It
was legendary what he could do with a block of
wood, and her father always thought he was wasting
his talent building houses instead of making furniture.

"Well, all your questions about Steele will be
answered shortly," Jason said, breaking into Jocelyn's thoughts. "He's due to show up any minute."

Jocelyn sneered. "And I can't wait for the illustrious Sebastian Steele to arrive."

Jason loosened his tie a little. He didn't envy the man one bit.

"Mr. Kilgore is expecting you, Mr. Steele. Just go right on in," Jason Kilgore's secretary said in a friendly voice.

Bas returned the older woman's smile. "Thanks."

He opened the door and glanced first at the older man sitting behind the desk who stood when he entered. Then out of the corner of his eye he saw that someone else was in the room and his gaze automatically shifted.

It was a woman and she didn't look too happy. She was definitely a beauty, with a mass of shoulder-length dark-brown curls that framed an oval honey-brown face with chocolate-brown eyes. Then there was the tantalizing fragrance of her perfume that was drifting across the room to him.

"Mr. Steele, I'm glad you made it. Welcome to Newton Grove," Jason Kilgore was saying.

Bas switched his attention from the woman and back to the man. "Thank you."

"So you're Sebastian Steele?"

Bas turned and met the woman's frown. "Yes, I'm Sebastian Steele," he answered smoothly. "And who are you?" he asked, although he had an idea. He could see Jim's likeness in her features, especially in the eyes. They were dark, sharp and assessing.

She crossed the room to stand directly in front of him, in full view, and he thought that she looked even better up close. She tipped her head, angled it back as if to get a real good look at his six-foot-three-inch form. And when she finally got around to answering his question, her voice was as cool as a day on top of the Smoky Mountains, and as unfriendly as a black bear encountering trespassers in his den.

"I'm Jocelyn Mason, and I want to know how you talked my father into leaving you a fourth of Mason Construction."

Jocelyn felt a tightness in her throat and couldn't help but stare at the man standing in front of her. No man should look this good, especially when he was someone she didn't want to like. And that darn sexy cleft in his chin really wasn't helping matters. Standing tall, he had thick brows that were slanted to perfection over dark-brown eyes that made you feel you were about to take a dive into a sea of scrumptious chocolate.

His cheeks were high with incredible dimples and his jaw was clearly defined in an angular shape. Then there was his hair—black, cut low and neatly trimmed around his head. And his lean masculine body had broad shoulders, the kind you would want to rest your head on.

Even with all those eye-catching qualities, there was just something captivating about him, something that showed signs of more than just a handsome face. His look—even the one studying her intently— had caught her off guard and she didn't like the way her heart was pounding wildly against her ribs or the immediate attraction she felt toward him.

Jocelyn took a quick reality check to put that attraction out of her mind and brought her thoughts back to the business at hand—Mason Construction Company.

"Well, aren't you going to answer, Mr. Steele?" she finally asked, her eyes narrowing fractionally. Inwardly she congratulated herself for getting the words past the tightness in her throat without choking on them.

He lifted a brow and said, "Yes, but first I must say that I'm very pleased to meet you, Jocelyn, and please call me Bas." He extended his hand. The moment she placed hers in his he liked the feel of it. How could a woman who worked in construction have such soft hands?

She pulled her hand away. "Now that we've dispensed with formalities, will you answer my question. Why did my father leave you part of Mason Construction?"

He held her gaze. "What if I told you that I had

nothing to do with it? Jim's decision was as much a surprise to me as it was to you and your sister."

Jocelyn considered his words. Leah hadn't been surprised. Nor had she been concerned. To Leah's way of thinking it had made perfect sense since she couldn't imagine Jocelyn running the male-dominated company alone. And as for Leah's share of the company, she had no problem with Jocelyn buying her out. She had other plans for her inheritance.

"Now that introductions have been made, can we all take a seat and get down to business?" Jason Kilgore said, halting any further conversation between Jocelyn and Bas. "I'm sure Mr. Steele would like to check into Sadie's Bed and Breakfast in time to take advantage of whatever she's fixed for lunch today. You know what a wonderful cook Sadie is, Jocelyn."

If Jocelyn did know she wasn't saying, Bas noted as he took his seat next to her in front of Jason Kilgore's desk. Her mouth was set in a tight line and he could tell she wasn't happy with his presence. *Furious* would probably be a better word.

He continued to study her, her cute perky nose and beautifully shaped mouth. He'd always been a sucker for a woman with sensuously curved lips. They were kissable lips, the kind that could easily mold to his.

"I was explaining to Jocelyn before you arrived

just what your function will be for the next couple of months, Mr. Steele." Jason Kilgore yanked Bas out of his reverie.

"And I was telling Jason that I thought Dad got you involved prematurely," Jocelyn quickly interjected.

"Do you?" Bas asked, noting just how dark her irises were.

"Yes. Dad taught me everything I know growing up and then he sent me to college to get a degree as a structural engineer. It was always meant for me to run the company."

"And you think I'm standing in the way of you doing that?"

"For a short while, yes, and as I said, it's all for nothing. When it comes to construction work, I can handle things."

A dimple appeared in the corner of Bas's mouth. For some reason he couldn't imagine her on a construction site, wearing a hard hat and jeans and wielding a hammer and saw while standing anywhere near a steel beam.

"And you find all this amusing, Bas?"

In a way he did, but he'd cut out his tongue before admitting it to her. There was no need to get her any more riled up than she already was. "No, Jocelyn, I don't."

"Good, then I hope you'll hear me out. I think it will save us a lot of time if you do."

Bas nodded. "All right. I'm interested in whatever you have to say."

"So, Bas, I hope you can see why you being here, keeping an eye on things, won't work."

Bas's lips curved into a smile. Although she had spent the last twenty minutes stating her case, trying to explain why his services weren't needed, he didn't see any such thing.

He glanced over at Jason Kilgore. The man had stopped fighting sleep—or boredom, whichever the case—and was leaning back in his chair and dozing quietly. Unlike Kilgore, Bas had given Jocelyn his full attention. It was hard to do otherwise.

First she had paced in front of him a few times, as if she'd needed to collect her thoughts. He, on the other hand, had needed to rein in his. The sunlight filtering through Kilgore's window had hit her at an angle that made her dark skin look creamier, her hair shinier and her lips even more tempting.

The woman had legs that seemed endless and the skirt she was wearing was perfect to show them off. Each time she paced the room, her hem would swish around those legs, making him appreciate his twenty-twenty vision. He loved what that skirt was doing for her small waist and curvy hips. And he couldn't help but notice the gracefulness of her walk. Her strides were a perfect display of good posture in motion and the fluid precision of a body that was faultlessly aligned.

"Bas, are you listening to what I'm saying?"

He heard the frustration in her voice and with a sigh he leaned back in his chair. "Yes, but it changes nothing. Your father asked me to return a favor. I owe Jim big-time and I believe in paying back any debts."

He knew his words weren't what she wanted to hear and her expression didn't hide that fact. "Mr. Steele, you are being difficult."

He lifted a brow. Since she hadn't gotten her way, it seemed he was Mr. Steele instead of Bas. "I'm sorry you feel that way, Jocelyn, but your father evidently felt the need for me to be here, otherwise he would not have added that stipulation in his will."

"And what about your ownership in the company?"

"What about it?"

"I'd like to buy you out."

That didn't surprise him. "I'll let you know my decision at the end of three months."

"Three months? But you only have to be here for six weeks."

He flicked a smile. "Your father's will indicated six weeks as the minimum period of time. If I recall, there was no maximum time given."

Anger shone in her features. "Surely you're not going to hang around here for three months?"

"Hey, keep it up, Jocelyn and I'll think you don't want me hanging around at all."

"I don't."

He shrugged. At least she was honest. "I'm sorry you feel that way."

"I see that our talk today didn't accomplish anything," she said.

Oh, he wouldn't go so far as to say that. Just watching her prance around Kilgore's office had accomplished a lot.

"What about your own company?"

She almost snapped the words at him, reclaiming his attention. Not that she'd ever fully lost it. "What about the Steele Corporation?" he countered.

"Shouldn't that be your main concern?"

He wished. "I left the company in good hands. My three brothers and my cousin know what they're doing," he said, thinking about Chance, Morgan and Donovan, as well as his cousin Vanessa, who handled public relations for the company. His other two cousins, Taylor and Cheyenne, pursued careers outside of the family business, although they served on Steele Corporation's board of directors.

"Besides," he decided to add, "it's time for me to take a vacation anyway." There was no need to elaborate on the fact that it was a forced one.

"By the time this is over, Mr. Steele, you're going to wish you had gone to Disney World instead."

"Possibly, but I'll take my chances. And what about your sister?" he decided to ask her. From her expression he knew immediately he'd hit a nerve.

She frowned. "What about her?"

"Are you buying her out?"

"Yes. She's never liked this town and I'm surprised she's still here. I expected her to return to California right after Dad's funeral."

He nodded. "After I get checked in at Sadie's Bed and Breakfast, I want to go over to the office and look around."

"I wish you'd consider my offer," she said.

"I can't do that."

Her eyes darkened. "In the end you're going to wish you had."

He stood, and when he took a couple of slow steps toward her, she had the good sense to take a couple of steps back. "I intend to carry out your father's request. That said, I think it will be in our best interest if we got along."

She glared at him. "I don't see that happening."

A tight smile spread across his face. "Maybe I should have told you that I like challenges, Jocelyn."

Chapter 2

Bas parked his car in front of Sadie's Bed and Breakfast and glanced around. He certainly hadn't expected this, all the changes that had taken place in Newton Grove since he'd last been here fourteen years ago.

It was still one of most beautiful, quaint towns he'd ever traveled to, but it no longer had that Mayberry look. He'd passed a Wal-Mart and Home Depot, certainly two things that hadn't been here before. And the library had been given a face lift. But the drive-in theater appeared to still be intact, as well as the Newton Rail Station that provided a memorable excursion up into the Smoky Mountains.

And from what he saw it was still a favorite place with tourists, which meant the souvenir shops that formed a tight circle in the town square were still thriving. The county fair, which was always held the third weekend in August, was a major event and always brought enough excitement to last the towns-people until the fall festival in the middle of November. He smiled, remembering all the stories Jim had told about both events. Boy, had he enjoyed hearing them.

Bas got out of the car and shoved his keys into the pocket of his jeans, appreciating Jason Kilgore for making arrangements for him to have a place to stay while in town.

Just being back in Newton Grove was stirring memories of how closely he had worked with Jim that summer, the bond they'd made and the special friendship that had been forged. He took a moment to lean against the fender of his rented car and glanced around, reflecting. In his mind he could actually see Jim loading lumber into his pickup truck while preaching to Bas in that strong, firm, yet caring voice. He'd told him the importance of a man being a man, about handling your responsibilities and taking advantage of every opportunity. The memory tugged at Bas's heart, and emotions swamped him. They were emotions that Jim had effectively shown him that it was okay to possess.

Bas suddenly blinked when the sound of a car's horn reclaimed his attention. Sighing deeply he went to the trunk to get out his luggage, thinking of his encounter with Jocelyn Mason. If the woman had her way he would be headed back to Charlotte by now. He could almost feel the daggers she had thrown in his back when he'd walked out of Kilgore's office.

He sighed again and glanced up toward the sky. "Jim, old friend, I hope you knew what you were doing because I don't think your daughter likes me very much."

"Aren't you that same young man who used to give us trouble?"

Sebastian glanced up from signing his name in Sadie's Bed and Breakfast's registration book and met the old woman's eyes. Something hard and tight settled in the pit of his stomach. It was a reaction he got whenever anyone recalled his less-than-sterling past.

If she had been someone from Charlotte, he would have shamefully admitted to it. But he distinctly remembered being on good behavior that summer while living in Newton Grove. For that reason he stared at her and said, "No, ma'am, you must have me mistaken for someone else."

Evidently she thought otherwise and her blue eyes sparked as she said, "No, I don't think so. I might be old—I'm pushing seventy—but I have a fairly good memory about some things. You worked with Jim, as part of his construction business one summer, over thirteen or fourteen years ago."

Bas's stomach began feeling unsettled again. She certainly did have a good memory. "Yes, but I didn't get into any trouble," he said defensively.

The old woman laughed. "Not any of your own making, trust me. But whenever you worked outside at a construction site on those extremely hot days, you drew an audience every time you took off your shirt."

She barked out another laugh and continued. "Yeah, I do remember that summer. You had all the young women acting like silly fools whenever they could take a peek at you. And I remember Marcella all but salivating whenever she saw you."

She studied him for a moment then said, "I understand you're going to be helping out at Mason's Construction again."

He took his Visa card out of his wallet to hand to her. News traveled fast in small towns. "Yes, ma'am, I am."

"I'm glad you saw fit to come help Jocelyn for a while now that Jim's gone. Lord knows she wouldn't ask for it, even if she needed it," Sadie went on to say. "And I'm curious as to what Leah's going to do. I expected her to leave town right after the funeral."

Bas put his charge card back into his wallet after

she returned it to him. "She lives in California, right?"

"So we hear. Leah left here at eighteen. She hated this place, claimed Newton Grove was too small town for her. She wanted to see the world and headed to California."

After a quick pause she added, "She broke Reese Singleton's heart when she left. They'd been sweethearts. He's a good man who didn't deserve what she did to him. You'll get to know Reese rather well over the coming months."

Bas leaned against the counter. "I will?"

"Yes, he's the foreman at Mason Construction. But he might not be there for too much longer."

Bas lifted a brow. "Why not?"

"Because he's better suited as a carpenter than a builder, and I heard that Jim left him a bunch of money to start his own business."

Bas turned to follow Sadie up the stairs to his room. Once he got settled he would check out what was happening over at Mason Construction.

The nail was taking a beating as Jocelyn hammered it relentlessly into the wood. A part of her wished it was Sebastian Steele's head.

If there was one thing she didn't need it was aggravation, and the man had gotten next to her like nobody's business. The nerve of him, thinking he could just waltz in and take over. Mason Construction was now hers and she would run things the way she saw fit, regardless of what he had to say.

It wasn't as though she didn't know what she was doing. Heck, she'd been reading blueprints practically since she could walk. Growing up, she'd spent hours at every job site with her father, learning each aspect of a builder's trade, from the ordering of the supplies to the overseeing of each structural design. While many construction workers had their specialties, Jocelyn was truly a jack-of-all-trades. She handled a paintbrush just as expertly as any artist; she could fit a pipe together as well as any master plumber, and she worked with brick, stone, concrete block and structural tile with the skill of an accomplished mason. For years she had worked alongside her dad and his crew as a fill-in, doing whatever task was needed and learning just about everything she could, before school, after school, weekends, whenever. She practically lived at Mason Construction except for those summer months when Jim Mason would ship her and Leah off to Aunt Susan in Florida.

Their mother's sister was as refined and proper as the words could get, and had been determined to pass those characteristics on to her nieces no matter how much they'd balked at the idea. After a while, Jocelyn and Leah discovered it was easier to just go with the flow and accept all the lacy, frilly dresses, the tea parties and the countless hours of walking with a book on their heads to perfect that graceful walk.

Now that she was a grown woman, Jocelyn appreciated her aunt's teachings and guidance to a degree she'd never thought would be possible as a young girl. She was glad she'd had the chance to express her gratitude to Aunt Susan before she died a few years ago. Jocelyn thought about the deaths of the three people who'd meant a lot to her—her mother when she'd turned sixteen; her Aunt Susan around six years ago and now her dad.

"If you keep beating that nail to death you'll whack it all the way through and bust up that board. Who ruffled your feathers today?"

Expelling a deep breath and clutching the hammer more tightly in her hand, Jocelyn decided Reese was right. There was no reason to take out her anger and frustration on a piece of wood.

She glanced up at him and knew he was waiting for an answer. It hadn't taken much for the men who worked for her to tell she was in a relatively foul mood, which is the reason they had been avoiding her. Reese had been at lunch when she'd arrived. Evidently the guys hadn't wasted any time giving him fair warning. Too bad all those deeply ingrained proper manners and stiff rules Aunt Susan had taught her weren't working for her today, especially the one about a lady not letting a man get on her last nerve, at least not to the point of showing it. A lady kept her cool and handled a man with charm and diplomatic grace.

Today, thanks to Sebastian Steele, all she could say to that notion was hogwash!

After leaving Jason's office she had gone home long enough to change into her work clothes, then joined the men at this particular jobsite. The only reason she hadn't been here at the crack of dawn like they had was because the mayor had requested her presence at a meeting in his office at eight. He liked being kept abreast of the plans for the city's Founder's Day Celebration next month, and since she was this year's chairperson, she had brought him up to date over bagels and coffee. And then there had been that ten o'clock meeting in Jason's office, the one she wished she could delete from her mind.

Jocelyn put the hammer down, deciding at the moment it was rather dangerous in her hand. "If you must know, Sebastian Steele is the person who ruffled my feathers. He has to be the most infuriating man I've ever met."

Reese smirked at her. "In other words, he wouldn't let you have your way with anything."

Jocelyn picked up the hammer again and hit it a couple of times in the palm of her hand. "You like your face, Reese?"

He grinned. "Yeah, I like my face, considering it's the only one I got."

And Jocelyn knew all the local girls thought it was a rather good-looking face, making him the most sought-after bachelor in town. But he was also the most elusive. She'd known Reese for six years, ever since his family had moved to Tennessee from Alabama when Reese was nineteen. The first time he'd seen her and Leah together out at the county fair, he had decided the then seventeen-year-old Leah, who was about to become a senior in high school, would one day be his wife. He was convinced he could erase the thought from Leah's mind of ever moving away from Newton Grove.

He'd been wrong and had gotten a broken heart to prove it.

"Well, if you like it so much, then knock it off. I'm not in a teasing mood."

"So I gather. Hey, this Steele guy can't be all bad since Jim thought enough of him to leave him part of the company."

Jocelyn frowned, narrowed her eyes, preferring not to be reminded of that. "Just because Dad liked him doesn't mean that I have to like him, too."

"No, but still I'd think you'd respect your father's wishes and try to make things work."

Jocelyn started hitting the hammer in the palm of

her hand again. "You're really making me mad. Don't you have something to do?"

Reese grinned. "Yeah, but I thought I'd come over here to make sure you'll be more help than a hindrance today. You know how I feel about going behind you and—"

Oh, that did it! He had really pushed her the wrong way, and just from the smile on his face she knew he was enjoying every single minute of getting her riled. She shot him a dark look. "Okay, just wait until you have to follow Steele's orders and see how much you like it."

Reese leaned against a window casement. "I don't mind following orders as long as they're solid and sound. And like I said Jim evidently trusted this man's judgment or he wouldn't be here."

"And it doesn't bother you that Dad didn't leave you a part of the company?"

The smile on Reese's face suddenly disappeared and he said in a quiet tone. "The only thing I ever wanted from your father was his baby girl. But that's history. Some days I wish I had never laid eyes on Leah."

Jocelyn nodded, understanding his feelings completely. Because of the four-year gap in their ages and the differences in their personalities, she and Leah hadn't been particularly close while growing up and she could never understand how her sister could walk away from a man who loved her as much as Reese had.

She waited, knowing Reese had more to say. For years he had kept his battered feelings locked inside, refusing to talk to anyone, even her father, about Leah and the hurt she'd caused him. But they'd known and accepted that the main reason Reese had joined the army within months of Leah's departure was to get away for a while. And he'd stayed away for two years.

"And why is she still hanging around? When is she returning to California?" he asked, with deep bitterness in his voice.

Jocelyn asked herself those same questions every morning when she awoke to find her sister still there. It wouldn't surprise her if Leah left during the night without saying goodbye. That was how she'd done it the first time. Her father had been devastated, Reese heartbroken and Jocelyn left wondering if she could have done something, anything, to improve their relationship while growing up, if she should have been less overprotective and smothering as Leah had claimed.

"I don't know why she's still here, Reese. A part of me would like to think she's finally decided to come home to stay, but I won't get my hopes up wishing for that one."

"And I'm hoping for just the opposite. I wish she

would leave and go back to wherever the hell she's been for the past five years."

Jocelyn felt Reese's pain and a part of her knew that even after all these years, he hadn't gotten over what Leah had done to him.

"Hope I'm not interrupting anything."

Jocelyn swirled around and her gaze collided with Sebastian Steele. She was surprised to see him, but should have known he would show up sooner or later. Her eyes narrowed. "Yes, your very presence is interrupting everything."

And with nothing else to say, she walked off.

No woman, Bas quickly decided as he watched Jocelyn cross the floor into what would be a master bedroom, should look that good in a pair of jeans. He scrubbed one hand across his jaw, pondering that phenomenon, as he continued to stare at her. He had found her utterly attractive earlier that day in a skirt and blouse, but seeing her dressed in work wear was having a more potent effect on him.

Well-worn jeans clung to her body like another layer of skin, but then gave a little with each step she took, providing a comfortable fit. Then there was her T-shirt, the one that boldly advertised Mason Construction across her chest, that made him appreciate, as he always did, a woman with a nice set of breasts.

The work boots and the bandana she wore around her head did nothing to detract from her femininity, and he had to concede that no matter what kind of clothes Jocelyn Mason wore, she was one of the sexiest-looking women he'd ever seen.

"I gather you're Sebastian Steele."

The man's words pulled Bas's attention back into focus and he shot him a curious glance. He had seen Jocelyn talking to him when he'd arrived, and the conversation had seemed pretty tense. Did the two of them have something going on more personal than business? "Yes, I'm Sebastian Steele."

The man studied him a moment and then said, "And I'm Reese Singleton, Mason Construction's foreman."

Bas remembered the name and everything Sadie had scooped him on earlier that day. This was the man who had gotten his heart broken by the other Mason female. He offered his hand. "Nice meeting you."

"The same here. I heard a lot about you from Jim."

"All good I hope," Bas said, returning his gaze to Jocelyn. He could tell from her body language that she was mad, from the way she was slapping the paintbrush against that wall as if she was brandishing a sword instead.

"She'll be fine. Jocelyn has a tendency not to stay mad for long."

Bas switched his gaze off Jocelyn and back to the man standing beside him—someone whose presence he had momentarily forgotten. Reese was grinning, his dark eyes flashing amusement behind the lenses of his safety glasses. "Is that right?" Bas asked, not liking the fact that Reese thought he knew Jocelyn so well.

"Yes, that's right," Reese said, hooking a thumb beneath his tool belt and leaning back against a solid wall. "I've known Jocelyn for almost six years now and her bark is worse than her bite. She's upset that her dad left you in charge of things for a while, and also that you got part of a company she felt was rightfully hers. But like I said, she'll get over it."

He studied the younger man and suddenly felt something he usually didn't experience with men other than his brothers—trust. For some reason, though, Bas knew that Reese Singleton was a man who could be trusted.

"I hope she gets over it because I have a job to do, one Jim left for me, and whether I want it or not, I plan to see it through. I owe him that much and more."

"Me, too," Reese said, following Bas's gaze as it moved to Jocelyn once more. "My family moved to the area when I was nineteen. I worked for Jim in the day and took college classes at the university at night. He replaced the father I lost at sixteen. He was my voice of reason when I didn't have one, my mentor and a good friend. At one point he stopped me from making a grave mistake, one that could have cost me my life."

Bas nodded. It sounded as if at one point he and Reese had been tortured by similar inner demons and in both situations it had been Jim who had helped to take them out of the dark and lead them into the light.

"How about if I introduce you to everyone?" Reese said, breaking into Bas's thoughts. "The sooner you know what's going on, the better. Right now everything's running smoothly but we can't expect things to stay that way since this is Marcella Jones's house we're presently working on and she's known to change her mind a lot. This is the third house we've built for her and her husband, and with this place she decided almost at the last minute that she wanted to add a huge lanai off her living room and bedroom. If nothing else changes, we'll be wrapping up things here in about three weeks."

"Thanks and yes, I'd like to meet everyone."

Bas glanced around as they made their way over to a group of men who were working on the cooking island that was part of the summer kitchen. Marcella Jones wasn't just getting a glass-enclosed lanai; she was getting a huge area that would be well suited for any and all her entertainment needs. He had to admit he liked the layout of the house and had admired each and every detail while passing through earlier.

The open-beam cathedral ceilings and the floor-to-ceiling windows would make the home light and airy, and provide a full mountain view no matter where you looked. In his mind he could see the finished product decorated with the finest of furnishings and beautiful art work.

Bas glanced over at Jocelyn and caught her staring at him. In that quick instance, something passed between them, and he felt it all the way to his gut. He frowned and told himself silently that the last thing he needed was to get interested in any woman, especially Jim's oldest daughter, no matter how tempting she was.

He had a job to do and he needed to get his mind on doing it and not on doing Jocelyn Mason.

Jocelyn swallowed back the knot that threatened to block her throat. Why did Sebastian Steele have to look so damn good? And those jeans he had on weren't helping matters one bit.

She gritted her teeth, wondering why she found him so attractive, then quickly decided his good looks and well-built body definitely had something to do with it. She jumped when she felt the mobile phone in her back pocket vibrate. Putting aside the paintbrush, she pulled the phone out. A quick check of the caller ID indicated it was Leah.

For the past five days, ever since the funeral, her sister had mostly spent her time going through their father's belongings and packing things up to give away. At first they had started doing the task together and then the memories had gotten too much for Jocelyn and she'd asked Leah to finish without her. Her sister had agreed. That was the one thing Jocelyn noticed about Leah since she'd been back. She was a lot more agreeable and less argumentative these days. There was a time when the two of them would disagree about almost anything, including the weather.

"Yes, Leah?"

"Just wanted you to know I cooked dinner and I thought it would be nice if we invited a guest."

Jocelyn moved her shoulders in a nonchalant shrug. She definitely didn't have a problem with Leah preparing dinner since her sister was a pretty good cook, but she did have a problem with the suggestion of a guest. She couldn't help wondering if Leah was finally going to come out of hiding and face Reese by inviting him to dinner. She had done a pretty good job of avoiding him the few times she'd returned home over the past five years.

"And just who will this dinner guest be?" she asked, curious as to how many languages Reese would say the words *hell no* in when he got the invitation from Leah.

"Jason called for you a short while ago and happened to mention that Mr. Steele arrived in town today."

"And what of it?" Jocelyn asked, leaning back against a wall she hadn't started painting yet.

"I think it would be a good idea to invite him to dinner. After all, he was Dad's friend."

"But that doesn't make him ours," she snapped, looking down at the hammer she had placed at her feet. She then glanced across the room at Bas. It was a tempting thought but she quickly decided that nothing and no one was worth going to jail.

"But I want to meet him. Aren't you curious?"

Jocelyn rolled her eyes. "I've met him and prefer not spending unnecessary time in his company."

"You've met him?"

"Yes."

"When?"

"Earlier today at Jason's office."

"Well, what do you think of him?"

Jocelyn glanced back across the room. Bas was staring at her and it annoyed her that she felt a quick tightening in her stomach. She wished she could blame it on something like indigestion but knew she couldn't. "There's no way I could sum up what I think of him in twenty-five words or less."

"I didn't ask you to."

Jocelyn couldn't help but smile. Now this was the Leah she was used to, someone always ready for a fight, and not the mousy person Jocelyn had picked up from the airport a couple of days before the funeral.

"Well, then," Jocelyn decided to say, "how about

infuriating, maddening, annoying, irritating, exasperating, galling—"

"Okay, okay, I get the picture, at least yours. I'd rather take my own snapshot and form my own opinion."

"Fine, then count me out."

"Aren't you being a little immature?"

That did it. Taking a slow, steadying breath, Jocelyn walked around the wall into a bathroom whose fixtures had yet to arrive. What she had to say to her sister needed to be said in private.

Closing the door behind her, she braced herself against the area where the pedestal sink would be and said rather heatedly, "How can *you* of all people fix your mouth to call anyone immature, Leah? I'm not the one who acted like a spoiled, immature brat by up and leaving home without as much as a goodbye, leaving her family worried for over a week before we finally heard from her."

Jocelyn knew now was not the time and place to unload feelings she'd held inside for years, but she'd done it and there was no way she could take back her words. Nor did she want to.

There was silence on the other end, and then Leah said in a somewhat quiet and unsteady voice, "There was a reason I left the way I did, Jocelyn, and maybe it's time I tell you why. At least that's what I've been told I should do."

Jocelyn felt an uncomfortable feeling in the center of her stomach. "Told by whom?"

"Look, I'll tell you everything when I'm able to talk about it, okay? Now getting back to Sebastian Steele, be forewarned. I do intend to invite him to dinner before I leave, Jocelyn."

"Leave? When are you leaving?" That uncomfortable feeling about being deserted by those she cared about was becoming unnerving. She lifted a hand to her chest, feeling a tug at her heart at the thought that she was losing her sister again, so soon after losing her father.

"I don't know, but I won't leave without telling you. I promise."

Before she could say anything, Jocelyn heard the gentle click in her ear. She took a deep breath. Her palms suddenly felt sweaty and she rubbed them against her jeans after returning the mobile phone to her back pocket. She had a feeling something was going on with Leah. But what?

She swung around when she heard the bathroom door swing open and her gaze collided with that of Sebastian Steele. She narrowed her eyes, madder than hell. "Don't you believe in knocking?"

He shrugged his broad shoulders as he leaned in the doorway. "I figured you couldn't be doing anything too private in here without any fixtures."

He was right, of course, but still. "Any closed

door is an indication that a knock is warranted before entering," she retorted.

He shook his head. "Save your rules for another time. We need to talk."

"We have nothing to discuss."

She made a move to walk past him when he said, "Reese just let Manuel go on my recommendation."

She stopped and swung around to him, nearly all in his face. "What?" she almost shouted at the top of her lungs, not caring her that her high-pitched voice didn't at all sound professional. "Manuel's the best and most dependable worker I have."

"Sorry, but you're going to have to find someone to replace him."

Jocelyn suddenly saw red, blood-red, and she fought the urge to go find her hammer and start knocking a few heads. First Bas's and then Reese's. She couldn't believe Reese had meekly followed Bas's orders without first consulting her. "How dare you think you can come in here and—"

"He's an illegal immigrant."

Jocelyn's mouth snapped shut and her gaze widened as if she'd been slapped by Bas's words. *Impossible* was the first word that came into her mind. Manuel had worked for her father for almost a year. There was no way Jim Mason would have broken the law by hiring an illegal immigrant. "I don't believe you. We have his citizenship papers on file at the office."

Bas then said easily, "Any papers you have are bogus. When I asked to see his green card, which is the same thing an inspector would have done had he shown up here, he got nervous and confessed the truth."

Jocelyn couldn't believe it. She didn't want to believe it. She shuddered at the thought of what would have happened if Duran Law had shown up. He was still plenty pissed about her continued refusal to go out with him. It seemed each time she'd turned him down his pride had gotten crushed. He would just love to hit her with a stiff fine and make her life miserable.

"And how did you know? I'm sure Manuel wasn't wearing a painted sign on his forehead," she all but snapped. A part of her was grateful Bas had saved her from possible misery under Duran's hands, but another part of her resented that he had discovered something she hadn't.

"I picked up on his nervousness when Reese introduced us. Trust me, in my line of work at the Steele Corporation, I'm faced with this fairly often enough. I wished there was a way around it but the law is the law."

She glared at him. "I know the law, Bas, and I don't have to trust you. But still, I appreciate you finding out about Manuel before I was faced with repercussions that I don't want or need. Thank you."

"No need to thank me. I was merely doing one of the things Jim brought me here to do."

And that was what bothered Jocelyn the most, knowing her father actually *had* brought him here and hadn't bothered to tell her. Jim Mason had been talking and in his right mind up to forty-eight hours before he'd died. Her father of all people knew that she didn't like surprises and should have told her about Bas.

"Fine," she said and began walking, annoyed when he automatically fell in place beside her. "That's a point for you. Now if you don't mind, I'd like to speak with my crew."

"They aren't here."

She stopped and stared at him as though he'd lost his mind. She quickly rounded the wall and looked around. "Where are they? It's only three o'clock. There's another hour of work time left."

Bas leaned back against an unpainted wall and crossed his arms over his chest. "I gave them the rest of the day off."

Jocelyn's mouth dropped. She wondered why it hadn't just fallen to the floor with his statement. "What do you mean you gave them the rest of the day off?"

"You would have done the same thing. Manuel has worked with these guys for almost a year. They're like family. All of them were shocked that he's in this country illegally, but they still felt bad that he won't be working with them any longer. They like him."

Jocelyn inhaled deeply. Bas was right. Now that

she thought about it, she *would* have done the exact same thing. "What's going to happen to Manuel? He has a family. A wife and child."

"Yes, and he also admitted to receiving public assistance benefits, public education for his son, public housing and other taxpayer-funded benefits over the past year without being detected."

Jocelyn glared. "You make him sound like a criminal," she snapped.

"Just stating the facts, ma'am. And something else you need to remember is that illegal immigration in this country is a crime that extends to anyone giving them a job."

"I know that, and I'm sure Dad didn't know he was an illegal. Like I said, Manuel's papers looked legit."

"I'm sure Jim didn't know. As for what will happen to Manuel, I have a feeling he'll be moving his family again. I agreed not to turn him in to the authorities."

Despite herself, she appreciated him for that. "Thank you."

"You're welcome."

For a long moment neither said anything else, but Jocelyn felt it just as clearly as if it was something tangible that she could reach out and touch. It was there, that same damn attraction she had felt from the first moment when her gaze had collided with his in

Jason's office. It was the same attraction that was there each time she'd stopped pacing on Jason's carpeted floor and found him staring at her with those intense dark eyes of his.

And it was there now as he leaned against the wall with his arms crossed over his chest, his head cocked to the side as if taking in the full view of her. A little more than a few feet separated them and whether she wanted to or not, she could feel his heat, and even at the distance she stood she could actually feel the warmth of his breath on her lips, coaxing her own to draw in his heat, mingle in his taste.

She inhaled deeply, thinking she must be losing her mind. She didn't want to be attracted to the man who owned a fourth of her company. The man who would be a pain in the butt for the next few months.

A man who had her stomach sizzling and intense heat gathering between her legs.

Drawing in another deep breath, she took a step back, started to move past him and stopped when he reached out and grabbed her wrist, gently pulling her closer, bringing her toe to toe, body to body.

"And another thing," he said huskily, before reaching out and lifting his hand to the knot in the scarf on her head. "I understand that on occasion you'll wear a hard hat or a scarf like this when there might be a lot of dust in the air. But just so you'll know, I really like seeing your head uncovered." And with that, he expertly took off her scarf, which made her curly locks tumble to her shoulders. And, as if he was satisfied with what he'd done, he then handed the scarf to her.

She balled it in her hand, crushed it while wishing it was his neck. Tilting her head, she glared at him. "I don't care what you like."

"Then maybe you should," he said, leaning in close, bringing his lips within a breathless inch. He smiled. "You have some temper and whenever I see you mad it makes me want to taste your anger."

Taste her anger? What he said didn't make sense because she didn't have a temper…at least not normally. Typically, it took a lot to make her mad. But she had to admit that for some reason he seemed to bring out the worst in her. When she opened her mouth to state that fact, he inched even closer and was within a heartbeat of closing his mouth over hers when the sound of a car door slamming had them quickly moving apart.

Jocelyn was grateful for the timely interruption before anything could happen. Something they would both regret.

"That's probably Marcella coming to check on today's work…as well as to make more changes. Goodbye, Bas," she said, moving swiftly past him and walking as fast as her legs could carry her.

Chapter 3

An entire week later, Jocelyn was still thinking about how close her and Bas's lips had come to touching. It would only have been a kiss, she'd tried telling herself over and over again. No big deal, she'd locked lips with other men before, although she could count on one hand the times she had done so.

Still, it annoyed her to no end that even after a week she could feel every muscle of Bas's body that had been pressed against hers. Then there had been his mouth, close, hot, ready. She could only imagine the taste of it. Her heart beat wildly in her chest at the mere thought. If Marcella hadn't shown up when

she had, there was no doubt in Jocelyn's mind that
they would have kissed.

Bas's face had been close to hers, breathing in her
scent the same way she'd been breathing in his.
Never had any man gotten absorbed in her senses so
quickly the way Sebastian Steele had. And then it
seemed that once Marcella arrived he had vanished
into thin air, leaving the job site by way of the back
entrance, making her wonder if the entire thing had
been real.

She had tried to avoid him, knowing he was
spending time at the office going through files and
records. She had no idea what he was looking for, but
as long as he stayed out of her way that was fine.
Twice she had seen him when she had stopped by the
office to sign some papers. He had been so wrapped
up in what he'd been reading that he'd barely acknowledged her presence, and she'd barely acknowledged
his.

"That pork chop is already dead, Jocelyn. There's
no need to keep stabbing it to death."

Jocelyn snatched up her head and met Leah's
gaze. Jocelyn had been so wrapped up in her
thoughts that she had completely forgotten her sister
was sitting across from her. They hadn't exchanged
a lot of conversation during dinner and eventually
their dialogue had drifted to a dead end.

Leah was nervous, Jocelyn could tell. If she had

been stabbing at her pork chop for the past few minutes, then Leah had been guilty of nervously nipping at her lips, an old habit when she knew she was about to get into trouble. Evidently Leah had something on her mind, something serious. Jocelyn wondered if her sister was ready to explain why she'd left home so abruptly. The explanation was five years too late, but then, better late than never.

She decided to go ahead and get the conversation started. "Last week you said you wanted to tell me something when you felt you could talk about it. Can you talk about it now?" Jocelyn asked, after taking a bite of her pork chop and savoring the taste. Evidently Leah had kept up her cooking skills during the five years she'd been away.

Whenever she'd come home—which had only been twice in five years—she'd only stayed for a couple days, as if passing through, and she never talked about why she had left Newton Grove or what she was doing in California. The only thing she would say was that she was fine and making it; she refused any money they offered her.

"Yes, I can talk about it now, but first tell me about Sebastian Steele. You haven't mentioned him at all this week."

Leah's request caught Jocelyn off guard and she had to fight not to choke on the piece of pork she was chewing. She quickly picked up a glass of water to wash it down. She had to be careful, very careful, not to give anything away, like the fact she found him so damn attractive and that they had almost kissed.

"I haven't had any reason to talk about him. He spends his days over at the office and I spend my time over at the job site. I haven't seen him much and that's the way I like it," she said.

At the lifting of Leah's brow it occurred to Jocelyn she really hadn't answered her sister's question. "All right, what is it that you want to know?"

"Well, when you talked about him he didn't seem like a nice person, which makes me wonder about his relationship with Dad. Why would Dad strike up a friendship with such a man as Sebastian Steele?"

Jocelyn could understand Leah's concern. She also knew it wasn't fair for her to portray Bas as a totally awful person. His handling of the Manuel situation had proven him quite the contrary, and had certainly earned him Reese's and the men's respect. He could have easily called the authorities and had Manuel arrested but he hadn't, and according to what she'd heard after talking to Reese later, Bas had even gone so far as to suggest that Mason Construction advance Manuel a full month's salary in recognition of his hard work and dependability.

Although it would be a lot of effort on her part, considering her dislike of Bas, she needed to convince Leah that even though she didn't know the full story, Bas was probably just the type of person her father would hook up with.

She leaned back in her chair and smiled. "I might have gone a little overboard in my description of him earlier," she finally said. "I was upset about the situation Dad placed me in with Mr. Steele and I immediately formed my own opinions of him. In the first few hours of our meeting I refused to consider that I might like him."

"And do you like him?" Leah asked, taking a sip of her tea and watching her sister closely.

Jocelyn reached for another dinner roll. "To say I like him would be stretching it a bit since I don't really know the man," she said honestly. "Let's just say I can tolerate him."

"How long does he have to hang around and supervise?"

"Dad's will indicated a minimum of at least six weeks. But Bas mentioned he would be around for at least three months."

"Bas?"

Jocelyn glanced up and saw the curious light shining in Leah's eyes and decided to put it out. She didn't want her sister getting any ideas about her relationship with Sebastian Steele. "Yes, Bas is what he prefers to be called. It's short for Sebastian."

"Oh, I see." After a few moments Leah added,

"I'm glad you'll be able to work with him, Jocelyn. And like I told you, I don't want my share of the business, so the sooner you can buy me out the better. I have plans for what I'm going to do with my money."

Although Jocelyn knew she didn't have any right asking, she couldn't help herself. "And what *do* you plan to do with it?"

To her surprise, Leah smiled and Jocelyn could see excitement shining in her dark-brown eyes. "I plan to open my own restaurant. For the past five years, I've been working as a cook while taking classes at a culinary school in San Diego to perfect the basics."

Jocelyn opened her mouth in astonishment. Leah had been working as a cook all this time? She didn't want to admit some of the things she'd wondered about what her sister was doing to stay alive. It had always been Leah's dream to hit California by storm and become a model. Jocelyn had heard just how unscrupulous some modeling agencies could be and had hoped and prayed that Leah hadn't gotten mixed up with one of them.

"What happened with your dream to become a model?" Everyone knew it had been Leah's aspiration. Everyone except for Reese. Oh, sure he'd known it, but he had counted on his love for her and her love for him changing her mind.

Jocelyn watched as Leah began nervously nipping

at her lips again. "I'd changed my mind about that
before I even left here."

Jocelyn frowned. Now she was confused. "Then
why did you leave the way you did? If you wanted
to become a cook you could have moved somewhere
close by. There are a lot of good restaurants in
Memphis and I'm sure Reese would have understood. Hell, considering how much he loved you, he
probably would have moved there with you. The two
of you could have made things work, Leah."

Jocelyn studied her sister, saw the tears that
suddenly sprang into her eyes and knew she'd hit a
sensitive nerve. "Yes, and believe it or not I had
decided on doing just that and was going to suggest
it to Reese, but…"

When Leah's voice drifted off and the tears began
pouring more freely, more abundantly, Jocelyn immediately got up and went to her sister, leaned down
and hugged her. "But what, Leah?" she inquired
softly. "If you had planned to hang around, why did
you leave the way you did and without telling anyone
you were leaving? Especially Reese?"

Leah shook her head, trying to regain her compo-
sure before she could speak. "Something happened,
Jocelyn, and I couldn't tell anyone. Especially not
Dad or Reese. Not even you."

Jocelyn heard the trembling in her sister's voice
and the strong conviction, as well. Whatever had

happened was something Leah actually thought she could not have shared with anyone. She pulled back and met her sister's intense, tear-filled eyes. "What happened, Leah?"

Leah hung her head for a moment, then when she lifted her gaze, Jocelyn saw in it tortured memories, recollections Leah didn't want to relive but was being forced to. Jocelyn felt a warning chill slowly work its way up her spine and thought that nothing could have been bad enough to make her sister flee into the night the way she'd done.

Jocelyn's hold on her sister tightened and she hoped she was giving Leah the strength to get out whatever it was she needed to say. When she felt Leah respond by holding tightly to her hand, she knew that she was. For the first time Leah was accepting all the smothering, the babying, the overprotectiveness she had refused from her for so many years.

"What happened, Leah?" Jocelyn inquired again, in an even softer tone of voice than before. "What happened to make you leave when you did?"

Leah opened her mouth to speak. Then paused. She slowly opened it again as she met her sister's intense stare. "I was raped, Jocelyn. Neil Grunthall raped me."

If Jocelyn had been standing upright instead of leaning over with her arms around Leah, she would have fallen to her knees. If not the words her sister had just spoken, then the pain and suffering she saw lining Leah's face would have definitely knocked her there. For a moment she began trembling, or was it Leah? No, she was certain it was her and she was trembling in anger.

"Neil raped you?" As she heard herself saying the words, she was stunned that the no-good drifter their father had hired on that spring had gone so far.

"Yes," Leah answered softly, "and please sit down. It's time I tell you about that time."

Jocelyn moved around the table, still clutching Leah's hand in hers, not wanting to lose the connection, the closeness, the need to exchange strength. When Jocelyn returned to her seat, she braced herself against the chair, needing support. "All right, tell me everything."

Leah lowered her head and whispered, "I doubt if I can, but I will tell you what you need to know, okay?"

At Jocelyn's nod of understanding, Leah began talking. "You know Reese and Neil never got along. Everyone wondered why Dad even hired Neil because he was nothing but a drifter and he was always causing trouble. Well, Dad finally fired him but I didn't know it. Late that same afternoon I went to the construction site looking for Reese. I wanted to tell him that I had decided to accept his marriage proposal and would go to a cooking school around here and wouldn't be moving to California after all."

A tear fell down Leah's cheek, joining the others. "I arrived at the job site, thinking the work crew was supposed to be there, working on Alyssa Calhoun's home. Instead I found Neil there, gathering up his stuff. I didn't know Dad had fired him just a few hours earlier. Neil claimed Reese was downstairs in the basement, finishing up something and stupid me, I went looking for him."

Jocelyn felt her sister's palms getting sweaty, but she held them tighter, refusing to let them escape her grasp. "And when he got me alone in the basement, he raped me and dared me to tell Dad or Reese. He said if I did he would deny it and convince Reese I went along with it."

"Reese would never have believed him, Leah, you know that."

"Yes, but nothing could erase the shame I felt after being taken like an animal on that floor. I felt humiliated, disgraced and dishonored. Reese had been the only man ever to touch me and I felt dirty and unworthy of him."

"So instead of telling anyone what happened, you left town," Jocelyn said, knowing that was exactly what her sister had done.

"Yes. If Reese had found out the truth, he would have killed Neil, if Dad didn't get to him first. And

I couldn't let that happen. Neither could I stand the thought of going to the police, pressing charges and facing the humiliation of Neil claiming it wasn't rape. You remembered what happened to Connie Miller when she claimed that one of the Banks boys raped her. She became the town's spectacle and eventually she and her family left disgraced."

Yes, Jocelyn remembered. Everyone had known that Ronnie Banks had done it, but the Bankses had had enough money to make Ronnie the victim instead of Connie.

"But it didn't necessarily have to turn out that way for you, Leah," Jocelyn said, though she clearly understood why her sister would have thought otherwise. Although Neil had been a drifter with no family ties to the area, it still would have been his word against hers. And with him being the trouble-maker that he'd been, and with his intense dislike of Reese, he would have loved to make it seem that Leah had practically begged for it.

It was through sheer will that Jocelyn didn't curse the ground the man was buried under. "If he weren't already dead I would find him and kill him."

Leah's trembling hands went still at the same moment she sucked in a deep breath. "Neil Grunthall is dead?" she asked in a shocked voice.

Jocelyn lifted a brow. "Yes, didn't you know? But then there was no way that you would have since you left town that same night. He left town drunk and drove to that tavern on the outskirts of town and got even drunker. It's my understanding that he was speeding, hit a tree and was killed instantly."

Leah hung her head and said softly, "I never knew that. The few times I came home I could never fix my lips to say his name to ever ask about him. It took me years just trying to deal with being a rape victim before admitting I needed help. I finally went to a victim assistance program and I discovered what I felt wasn't unusual. A rape victim feels ashamed, weak and wounded, and unless they get help they will continue to feel that way. The program I got into has helped me to come to terms with what Neil did, but I have some ways to go before fully recovering. Even to this day I haven't been able to let another man touch me intimately."

"Oh, Leah," Jocelyn said, tightening her hand around Leah's. "You shouldn't have gone through that alone. Even if you didn't want to confide in Reese and Dad, then what about me? You could have come to me."

Leah shook her head. "No, I couldn't have, Jocelyn. You were the one who always did the right thing. You would have gone straight to Dad and told him what happened and I couldn't risk you doing that. Neil was crazy and there was no way I was going to tell Dad or Reese what he'd done."

For a long moment neither of them said anything, and then Jocelyn quietly asked the question she needed to know. "Are you going to tell Reese?"

Leah met her sister's intense stare and shook her head. "No. I still can't stand the thought of Reese ever finding out what happened, Jocelyn, and I don't want his pity. This is something I have to overcome in my own way and time. Like I told you earlier, I can't stand the thought of a man touching me that way. I can barely tolerate the times I have to visit the doctor for my physicals. Besides, I hurt Reese in a way he would never forgive me for."

"Yes, but if knew the truth about why you left, then he—"

"No, Jocelyn, I won't tell him. It doesn't matter now because I can't ever be that way with a man again even if he did understand. So it doesn't matter. I won't tell him and I want you to promise me that you won't ever tell him, either."

Jocelyn turned her head and gazed out the window. She knew how much Leah leaving without a word had hurt Reese, so much, in fact, that he had left town for a couple of years to get over it. Once he had served time in the army he had returned, and barely ever mentioned Leah's name. Jocelyn had been nervous as to what his reaction would be upon seeing Leah again at their father's funeral. She had watched him, had studied his expression the exact moment Leah had walked into the church. Jocelyn had seen the pain and the hurt that was still there, that five years hadn't fully erased.

"Jocelyn, you have to promise me."

Jocelyn turned and met her sister's pleading gaze. Then she remembered the reason Leah hadn't come to her the night she'd been raped was that she'd known that no matter what, Jocelyn would have done the right thing and told her father anyway. There was no way she would have let Neil get away with hurting her sister.

And although she didn't agree with what Leah was asking her to do, it was her sister's decision to make, and she would do as she asked. "I promise. I won't tell Reese, but I'm hoping that one day you will."

There weren't too many places to go in Newton Grove when you wanted to get away for a spell, but Jocelyn was determined to find one.

When she came to a traffic light she stopped and rubbed the bridge of her nose with her fingertips, recalling what Leah had shared with her at dinner. Each time she thought of her sister being powerless under the hands of Neil Grunthall, she literally felt sick to her stomach. And to think Leah had endured alone the humiliation of being raped.

She sighed, feeling tears sting her eyes. Now everything made sense and she felt angry with herself for not having known something hadn't been right. Before she'd disappeared, Leah had stopped talking about leaving Newton Grove. In fact her relationship with Reese had grown that much more serious. But Leah hadn't shared with Jocelyn her decision to marry Reese. If she had, then Jocelyn would have known for certain that something was wrong when she just up and left town.

After dinner she and Leah had tidied up the kitchen together, then, as if she'd needed to be alone, Leah had taken a shower and gone to bed early. Jocelyn had needed to go somewhere and take out her anger and frustration on someone, anyone, and for the past hour had been riding around town trying to cool down.

It was times like this that she missed her dad something awful. He would have known just what to say to Leah. Then there was the issue of Leah not telling Reese. Jocelyn thought Leah was making a big mistake by not doing so.

Not having any particular place to go, but knowing she wasn't ready to return home yet, she turned the corner toward the office where Mason Construction was located.

Jocelyn's hands tightened on the steering wheel when she pulled into the yard and slipped into the space right next to a car already there. She recognized the dark-blue sedan and immediately the anger she had tried cooling for the past hour rushed back in full force. What was Sebastian Steele doing at the Mason Construction office at nine o'clock at night?

Barely waiting for her car to come to a complete stop, she quickly unsnapped her seatbelt and then yanked open the car door. There couldn't be that many files that he had to go over to be practically spending the night here. Angrily, she grabbed her purse before slamming the car door shut. Just what was he looking for in those files anyway?

When she reached the top step, she could see through the glass door his profile as he sat at the conference table, and without even thinking of surprising him, she snatched open the door and then slammed it shut.

He turned from the papers he'd been reading and looked at her. And at that moment she wished he hadn't. There was just something about those dark eyes whenever they lit on her that prompted an overpowering sensation to slide all the way up her spine. Of course she was imagining things but for a moment she thought she felt the floor move. Still, to retain her balance, in case she hadn't imagined it at all, she tightened her fingers on the strap of her purse and placed pressure on the soles of her feet when he stood up.

He was wearing jeans and a black T-shirt. She hated admitting it, but he looked good in black. It did something to the darkness of his eyes and the tone of his complexion. Just looking at him was such a mind-boggling experience that for a moment she forgot what she was upset about. Until a half smile curved his lips.

Then she quickly remembered.

"What are you doing here, Bas?"

Instead of answering her, he said, "I'm curious about something, Jocelyn."

At the moment she didn't give a flip what he was curious about and was hoping her expression told him so. Evidently not, since he then added, "Are you always in such a pleasant mood?"

She gave him a stony look, one that could probably solidify cement in an instant. "You're going to see just how pleasant I can be if you don't answer my question. What are you doing here? This office closes at five o'clock."

His smile widened. "My work hours aren't dictated by a clock. And as to what I'm doing, I'm still working."

She glanced at the papers spread out on the table and the stack of files on one of the chairs. She then looked back at him. "Why?"

He lifted a brow. "Why what?"

"Why are you here working this time of night? And not only that, why do you feel the need to? You just got here a week ago."

"Let's just say I'm an eager beaver. I believe in getting the job done."

Angrily, she shook her head and said, "But there isn't a job here to do. You can go through whatever you want, but you'll find everything is in order. Like I've said, there is no reason for you to be here."

"And my response to that is still the same," he said, taking his seat back at the table. "Evidently your father thought otherwise."

That statement, as usual, triggered Jocelyn's anger to the boiling point. She crossed the room and slapped her hands, palms down, on the table and leaned in toward him. Their lips were within inches of touching.

She opened her mouth to speak, but he beat her to it. "Be careful about getting too close, Jocelyn. I'm liable to bite." And then in an even lower voice, he added, "I'm also known to lick, nibble, taste, sample. Should I go on?"

Bas watched as a deep color rose in her cheeks when she got the picture he'd painted. Unfortunately for her she didn't pull back quick enough and when she unconsciously tilted her head at an angle that brought her mouth even closer, Bas decided to carry out his threat. She was mad anyway, and a little more anger wouldn't make or break their already fiery relationship.

He locked his mouth to hers before either of them could take their next breath. And he felt her fingers reach out and curl into his shirt the exact moment his tongue entered her mouth. He heard her moan, not

in protest but in surrender, and the sound spurred
him on.

He had never indulged in a kiss that had made him
forget his senses so quickly and so easily. He might
have initiated it, but she was certainly adding a delicious topping.

From the taste of things it seemed that he was way
over his head and sinking fast without any thoughts
of a rescue. But there was only so much of Jocelyn
Mason's passion he could take, and, after giving her
tongue one final, passionate suck, he hesitantly
pulled back. His gaze stayed glued to her features,
and he saw she was dazed and for the moment
speechless. But not for long.

"How dare you," she murmured angrily between
moist lips.

"How dare I what? Kiss you or stop kissing you?"
he asked, leaning in a little closer. When she didn't
speak up quickly enough for him, he clamped his
mouth onto hers again, intent on showing her that he
did dare, because from her response it was obvious
that she was enjoying the exchange as much as he
was. This time he savored her taste at a slow pace,
licking, nibbling and tasting. He soon discovered
that kissing her slowly wasn't a good thing because
he didn't want to stop. There was something deeper,
different, in her taste this time around. It was more
succulent, heated, and it had him devouring her lei-

surely, at an unhurried pace, yet greedily, as if once the taste was gone, that would be it. It was either now or never.

He heard her protesting moan when he finally pulled back again. "Got enough or do you want more?" he whispered, finishing her off by taking his tongue and lining the outside of her lips.

"Enough," Jocelyn said softly, shaking her head as if to clear any lingering passion that had gotten lodged in her brain. His kiss was everything she'd somehow known it would be and then some. She could only stare at him in amazement and wonder. How many practice sessions had he endured to become a fantastic kisser?

Deciding she was better off not knowing, she leaned back and took a step away from the table. She would certainly think twice before she ever got in his face again. Although the kiss had whopped her senses, all it took was seeing the files and folders he'd been going through to make her recall that she was still angry at him for being here.

She crossed her arms over her chest. It was either that or be tempted to reached out and grab him for another kiss. Jeez, what was happening to her? She might not have asked for his kiss but she had wanted it, and would shamefully go so far as to admit that she had anticipated his taste since meeting him.

"I need to know something," Jocelyn said slowly,

struggling to understand why her father had thought
Sebastian Steele was needed here.

He glanced up at her. "What?"

"Is there anything in particular you're looking for
here? Did Dad give you any indication that something is wrong with the business? Something that I
don't know about? Something that he didn't want
me to know?"

Bas shrugged his broad shoulders and his gaze
was level and calm when he responded, "No."

She lifted a brow. "Then explain the reason you're
here, because until I understand it, I will continue to
fight you at every turn. Dad hadn't been able to run
the company for the past eight months. The chemo
treatments took a toll on him. I've been in charge of
things practically since the first of the year when the
cancer was diagnosed, so why did he bring you in?
Didn't he think I could handle things here?"

Bas leaned back in his chair. Evidently she didn't
understand what he did for a living and the way he
could benefit Mason Construction during the short
time he'd be here. He held up his hand when she
started talking again.

"First of all, let me assure you that my being here
has nothing do to with your father's lack of confidence
in your abilities, Jocelyn. Over the years, whenever I
spoke to Jim he was always singing your praises and
telling me what a great job you were doing."

What he had just told her was the truth and for some reason it was important to him that she believed what he said. He then decided to lean in closer to make sure she was taking in his every word. "I'm a troubleshooter, Jocelyn. Some corporations refer to us as consultants. After I dropped out of college I did a lot of odd jobs, working various places, so I had an in-depth knowledge of organization and customer support services. Your dad convinced me to return home, go back to school and become a part of my family business. When I did return to college, I concentrated on those areas I needed to polish and then went to work full-time with my dad and brothers at our company. My job is to avert trouble before it can cripple a corporation, whether it's in employee relations or customer services." Giving her a confident smile he said, "And at the risk of sounding cocky, I'm pretty damn good at what I do."

He motioned to the files he had spread out around him. "Already I can see several areas within Mason Construction that are red flags."

He knew she wouldn't like his observation. He saw the slow flaring of her nostrils, the way her eyebrows lifted ever so slightly, the way her lips turned down faintly. Maybe he was a sicko or something, but seeing the heat rise in her cheeks was actually turning him on. Was that crazy?

"What red flags?"

He studied her features and saw the fire in her eyes and the pout of annoyance around her mouth. He wanted to reach out and skim his fingers across those lips he had kissed just moments ago. Damn, but he really liked her mouth, the shape, texture and taste.

"Bas, I asked you, what red flags?"

His focus returned to her question with the sound of her impatient foot tapping against the hardwood floor. Not to get her dander up any more, he decided to answer. "Like this job for Marcella Jones for instance."

The name of the woman who had that very afternoon given her even more changes to make caused Jocelyn to flinch involuntarily. "What about the Marcella Jones project?"

"All those changes are costing the company money and you didn't allow for them."

She absently rubbed the back of her wrist as her eyes narrowed. "There's no way you can allow for them. Marcella makes changes. A builder gets to live with it. Everyone knows it and accepts it."

"But why should you?"

Jocelyn breathed deeply. Unfortunately she was finding Bas's voice sexy, which was something she didn't like. She needed to stay focused on what they were discussing. "Because the contract pays big bucks. I've padded for some anticipated changes but there's no way I can cover all of them. Everyone knows Marcella is a builder's nightmare."

"I suggest you handle it differently."

Jocelyn's eyes narrowed again. "And just how do you suggest I handle it?"

"Let her know that with changes come surcharges because they're costing you time and money. Once you hit her with enough surcharges, she'll lighten up."

Jocelyn laughed. "What she'll do is drop us like a hot potato."

"I don't think so."

The only thing he had in his favor in making that statement, Jocelyn thought, was that he didn't know Marcella. "And why wouldn't she?"

"Because she would want the best outfit building her home, someone she knows will do it right. You said this isn't the first home you've built for her, right?"

"Yes, it's the third."

"Then there's a reason she keeps coming back."

"Yes, to get on everyone's last nerve."

"But at some point it has to stop. I suggest we try it. The next time she makes changes tell her Mason Construction has implemented a new policy and then explain the surcharges to her."

Jocelyn hated admitting that what he was suggesting sounded reasonable, but as she'd told him earlier, Marcella would never go along with it. Her family had money, the man she'd married had money, and she liked to flaunt that fact. She was used to getting anything she wanted, no matter whom she inconvenienced.

"Like I said, it won't work."

"Try it. What do you have to lose?"

"Her business."

Bas chuckled. "I doubt if she would do anything that drastic this late in the building phase."

Jocelyn sighed deeply. She didn't relish the thought of Bas meeting up with Marcella, given her reputation as a married woman with a roving eye. But Jocelyn quickly decided that Bas was old enough to handle his own business and he deserved a confrontation with someone like Marcella. It would be the first real test he'd fail.

"Fine, if you want to tangle with Marcella then go right ahead, but don't say I didn't warn you," she tossed over her shoulder as she moved down the hall.

When she got to her office, she closed the door behind her, immediately dismissing Marcella from her thoughts. Instead she thought about the kiss she'd shared with Bas. Okay, they had kissed and it was out of her system. She licked her lips still moist with his taste. Out of her system? Not by a long shot.

Chapter 4

Bas tossed aside another folder before looking at his watch. It was close to midnight. He'd accomplished a lot in his first week and felt pretty good about it. As he'd told Jocelyn, already he'd come across several red flags. Luckily, none of them were major and all could be taken care of before they reached problem status.

And speaking of Jocelyn...

He frowned at the stillness, the silence, the complete lack of sound. At one point during the night he had heard the keys of a computer clicking, the opening and closing of file cabinets and the soft hum of a song from a feminine voice. But now he heard nothing and since she would have had to pass him to leave, he could only assume she was still here. And if she was, just what the heck was she doing?

Curiosity had him standing and making his way down the narrow hallway. The door to her office was ajar and he could see that the room was crammed with a desk, a computer and several file cabinets, not to mention a number of healthy-looking green plants. He knocked.

"Come in."

He pushed the door open the rest of the way and stepped inside, glancing around. Jocelyn was stretched out on a sofa, flat on her stomach, in a comfortable position. And she was…coloring. He blinked, certain he was seeing things, but he wasn't. She had a thick coloring book and a huge box of crayons in front of her and was diligently at work. Instead of a twenty-seven-year-old woman, she reminded him of a ten-year-old.

All it took was a look at those serious curves outlined beneath her jeans and blouse to know she was definitely no kid; however, there was something about her gliding that crayon across the page that gave her an air of innocence. At that moment some unknown force crept into him and he was touched by a degree of tenderness he experienced only on very good days and then solely for certain people. Unable to help himself, he crossed the room and stared down at her for a moment. "What are you doing?"

She glanced up as if annoyed at the interruption. "What does it look like? I'm coloring." She then turned her attention back to her paper.

"Okay," he said, as if the reason made perfect sense. He decided to press further by asking, "Why?"

She didn't bother to look up when she responded. "Why what?"

Now he was getting annoyed. "Why are you coloring in a book at midnight? In fact, why are you coloring at all?"

She pushed the coloring book aside and pulled herself up to a sitting position. "I'm coloring because it's something I like doing. Always have. It relaxes me."

She studied him for a moment then asked, "Isn't there something you used to do as a kid that you've carried into your adult life?"

Bas thought long and hard then answered. "Yes, now that I think about it, there is something."

"What?"

"Basketball. My brothers and I grew up playing basketball together, and we still do every Saturday morning, although now we do it for a different reason. It's no longer just for fun."

Jocelyn lifted a brow. "What is it for now?"

He smiled. "To leave our egos on the court." At

the confused expression that crossed her features, he
decided to explain.

"I have three brothers and all of us work at the
Steele Corporation. We're different in personality
and temperament, and it's not easy for us to work
together because of our strong differences of
opinions. Playing a game of basketball every
Saturday morning helps get rid of any competitive
frustrations we might have before the start of a new
week. I'm really going to miss not being there to do
that," he said, chuckling. "It will give Morgan a
chance to elbow someone else in the ribs for a
while."

"Um, sorry you'll be missing the game each
week, but if you're nice I'll let you borrow my crayons," she said teasingly.

"Thanks but I'll pass."

"Hey, coloring is fun, so don't knock it," she said,
placing a playful pout on her lips.

Looking at her mouth Bas couldn't help but think
about the kiss they had shared earlier. Now *that* had
been fun. Kissing her had been such a delicious,
intimate contact and had proven him right. She did
have kissable lips. The moment he had coaxed her
tongue into his mouth and latched on to it for all it was
worth, he'd thought he'd actually felt the ground
shake. The softness of her tongue had made him want
to continue kissing her, the taste of her had tempted

him to do more. Self-control eventually made him end
the kiss. And that same self-control was keeping him
from leaning in close and reclaiming her mouth now.

"And you probably don't watch cartoons either,
do you?"

Her question intruded into his thoughts and he
figured that was a good thing, since what he'd been
thinking was liable to get him in trouble. "No, I don't
do cartoons, either."

"Not even *Finding Nemo?*"

"Didn't know he was lost, so no, not even
Finding Nemo."

He watched her shudder as if the very thought of
anyone not having seen that particular movie was incredible. Pretty much the same way he felt about
anyone not eating Kentucky Fried Chicken.

"So tell me, Sebastian Steele, just what do you do
for fun?" she asked, regaining his attention.

"Fun?"

"Yes, fun. You know, the activity that you're
supposed to do when work ends."

"Work for me doesn't end. I enjoy what I do."

"I enjoy what I do too, but not 24/7. Come on, get
with it. Everyone is entitled to some fun time to just
unwind, regroup and relieve stress. Don't you believe
in work/life balance?"

Bas chuckled. Work/life balance? Was there really
such a thing? She was beginning to sound like his

brothers, who thought too much work with no playtime was a deadly sin. If that was the case, then he was looking hell straight in the face, since he was used to working into the wee hours of the morning. As long as he could grab a few hours of sleep and wake up the next morning to a decent-tasting cup of coffee, then he was good to go.

Knowing that she was waiting for a response, he said, "I get my work/life balance when I go to sleep."

"Oh. And how many hours do you sleep each night?"

He was beginning to dislike her questions. "I get enough sleep. And speaking of sleep, it's late and I was about to leave."

"Okay. Good night."

He raised a brow and shoved his hands deep into the pockets of his jeans. "Aren't you leaving, too?"

"No, I plan to hang around awhile and color a few more pages," she said, brushing aside a curl that had fallen on her cheek.

He frowned, not liking her answer and not liking the fact that he was tempted to reach out and curl that lock of hair around his finger and tilt her mouth to his and…

Damn. He quickly sucked in a deep breath, determined to bring his heated thoughts back on track. He then forced himself to concentrate on what she had said about not leaving yet. There was no way he was going to leave her here alone at this time of night. "What's your day like tomorrow?"

"Since we can't do anything at the Jones place until the inspector gets there to check things out, which probably won't be until after lunch, I'm going to be at school in the morning."

He cocked his head to one side, trying to figure out what she was talking about. "School? Are you taking a class or something? "

"No. I offer my assistance to several schools where they need more help in the classrooms. Budget cuts have made smaller class sizes impossible, so I do what I can to help out. It's something I enjoy doing. For me it's another fun activity. And then at noon I have a business meeting." She raised her hand over her head as if to stretch the kinks from her upper body.

He tried not to notice how the stretching made her blouse tighten over her firm breasts. He cleared his throat. "Sounds like you have a rather full schedule tomorrow, which is all the more reason you should go home and get a good night's sleep. Let's go."

When she didn't move and sat there glaring at him, he lifted a brow. "Is there a problem?"

"Yes, there's a problem," she said, standing and placing her hands on her hips. "First of all, let's get a few things straight right now. You are not my keeper so don't tell me when to go or when to stay. Secondly,

I don't like interruptions during what I consider my fun time, and thirdly, why should you care about how much sleep I get? Your concern should be with Mason Construction, and I hope you'll do what you came here to do then leave before getting too underfoot."

"Too underfoot?" he growled, not liking what she'd just said. In record speed he crossed the room and before she could blink, he had her backed up against a wall, his body pressed intimately to hers. "You wouldn't know underfoot if it bit you, Jocelyn. *This* is underfoot," he said heatedly, roughly, with more than a tinge of anger. "And yet this isn't as close as it can get."

He leaned in closer and whispered across her lips. "Don't push me," he warned huskily. "Especially for all the wrong reasons."

She frowned, refusing to back down. "With you there won't be any right reasons. And if I didn't make myself clear the first time then I'll repeat myself. You don't tell me what to do."

Bas inhaled deeply. For some reason she was itching for a fight, but he wasn't in a mood to accommodate her tonight. And she had no idea how close she was to being thoroughly kissed again. However, with her temper flaring, he knew better than to try it, although he couldn't stop the images flashing through his mind of all the other things he would love doing to her. Since he hadn't slept with a woman in over eight months he was horny as hell and it wouldn't take much to tumble her back on that damn sofa and seduce the hell out of her. But he had to remember the key element he'd learned and one he hadn't grasped during his teen years—discipline. He knew how to pull back and behave properly when he needed to, and this was one of those times.

His eyes met hers and he gazed into their angry depths. But he was experienced enough to see beyond the anger and notice something else, something she was trying like hell to fight—deep longing, need and heated desire. Those were the last things a man in his predicament needed to see in a woman's eyes.

Mustering his self-control and discipline, he took a step back. "Look, it's been a long and tiring day. How about if we call a truce tonight and go get some sleep, okay?"

Jocelyn sighed. Although she didn't like admitting it, Bas was right. It *had* been a long and tiring day, and having to deal with what Leah had told her had definitely taken a toll. Besides, she heard the weariness in his voice and if sleeping was the only way he got his work/life balance, then she definitely didn't want to stand in his way.

"Okay, I'll leave but only because I want to and not because you told me to," she said, putting away her coloring book and crayons.

"Here, take this. The temperature has dropped quite a bit since you got here," he said, taking off his jacket and placing it around her shoulders before she had time to protest. But he saw the stubborn set of her chin and the indecision that lit her eyes, and for a moment he wondered if she would snatch his jacket off. He was a little surprised when she said, "Thanks."

"You're welcome."

After locking up, they walked to their cars together, neither saying anything. After opening her car door and sliding behind the steering wheel, she was about to remove his jacket when he said, "No, you can keep it. I have another one."

When she opened her mouth to say something, he held up his hands and chuckled. "A truce remember? And it's too late to argue."

She nodded. "Fine, but I'll give it back to you tomorrow."

"Do whatever you want and drive carefully tonight."

Jocelyn watched while he walked to his own car, trying not to notice the way his jeans covered firm, muscular thighs and a too-fine butt. The tingle that suddenly spread through her was so strong that her grip tightened on the steering wheel and her breath whooshed out from her lungs.

She pulled herself together, and as she switched on the ignition she inhaled deeply to get her breathing back right again. Moments later she noted that he had no intentions of pulling away until she did. Glancing down at the black leather jacket, the one with the strong scent of man, she breathed in deeply once again. She'd had every intention of giving back his jacket when he had first placed it around her shoulders, but then the alluring aroma was absorbed into her nostrils at the same time her body was flooded with soothing warmth, and she'd decided to keep it on. The man could certainly be a gentlemen when he wanted to be.

"Okay, he's nice but I still don't like him," she muttered out loud.

And as she backed out of the parking space and headed toward home, she had to reaffirm her dislike for him several more times.

"Are you taking your medicine like you're supposed to, Bas? What about getting an adequate amount of rest? Are you eating right?"

Bas shook his head as he wandered out of the bathroom, where he had just finished taking a shower, and into the bedroom. After awakening this morning and downing his first cup of coffee, he'd figured he would have a pretty good day...at least he'd thought so until the phone rang. Before he could say hello, his sister-in-law was bombarding him with questions.

"Did Chance put you up to calling me, Kylie?" he asked, sitting on the edge of the bed. The sunlight was pouring in through the window and in the far distance he could see the Smoky Mountains.

"No, I'm just concerned about you."

"I've only been gone a week."

"Yes, but you know what a worrywart I am. Besides, Chance and I want to tell you our news."

Bas lifted a brow. "What news?"

He could hear her throaty laugh. "Here's Chance. I'll let him tell you." He heard her handing over the phone to his brother.

"Bas?"

Bas leaned back against the headboard. "Okay, Chance, what's going on? What's this news you and Kylie have to tell me?"

"Nothing major. Just the fact that you're going to be an uncle...again."

A huge smile spread across Bas's face. His brother had remarried eight months ago after being a widower for seven years. "Hey, that's wonderful. Congratulations. How do the kids feel about the upcoming addition to your household?" By kids he meant Kylie's fifteen-year-old daughter, Tiffany, and Chance's sixteen-year-old son, Marcus.

"They're thrilled and already fighting over baby-sitting rights." Chance laughed. "I'll see how eager they are for the job when the baby arrives and they find out what changing diapers is all about."

Bas talked to his brother for another ten minutes, filling him in on how things were going. "So, Jocelyn Mason wasn't glad to see you, huh?" Chance asked.

"Nope, not that I figured she would be."

"She sounds like a handful."

Bas smiled. Yes, she was a handful all right, but at the moment he thought of her being a mouthful. At three in the morning he'd been wide awake remembering just how good that sassy mouth of hers had tasted. Even now the memory shot his pulse up a notch or two. And then there was the luscious scent of her perfume that he was convinced had gotten absorbed into his skin, since he could still smell her.

"Yes, she's a handful for now, only because she sees me as a threat. Once she sees that I'm only here to help, she'll be okay," he said with more confidence than he really felt.

"I hope you're right. The last thing you need is to get stressed about anything."

"Trust me, Chance. The last thing I'd do is let any woman stress me out. You should know that about me."

After a few more minutes of small talk with his brother and sister-in-law, who reminded him of the surprise party next month for his brother Donovan's birthday, Bas hung up the phone then stood and walked over to the window and looked out. What he'd told Chance was the truth. He didn't plan on letting any woman stress him out. If Cassandra Tisdale hadn't done it during the six months of their engagement then such a thing wasn't possible.

He smiled as he checked his watch. It was time for his workday to begin.

Jocelyn glanced over at the man sitting across from her and smiled. "I'm flattered by your interest in Mason Construction but it's not for sale, Mr. Cody," she said, sipping a glass of lemonade.

What she had told him was the truth. She was truly flattered. She had read enough articles in *Black Enterprises* to know that if Cameron Cody was looking at any company to add to his portfolio then there was a good reason for it, because he was fast becoming a powerhouse. He was a high-school dropout who had eventually gotten his act together to later graduate cum laude from Harvard Business School, and now, at thirty-four, he was one of the most success African-American men in the country.

Cameron Cody was a self-made millionaire who had a knack for investing in all kinds of profitable ventures. His latest was construction, after he, along with other noted celebrities, had combined their funds and formed a construction company to help rebuild communities in New Orleans destroyed by Hurricane Katrina. The success of that venture had given him the idea to purchase a number of construction companies in various parts of the country to build low-income housing. Jocelyn thought his idea was good as well as needed. But as she'd told him, Mason Construction was not for sale.

"If you change your mind," Cody said, going into his pocket to pull out a business card, "please let me know. The offer will stand. The task force I put together was thorough in providing me with the names of construction companies around the country that have good, solid reputations. You should be proud that your company is one of them. That speaks highly of your leadership."

Jocelyn smiled, placing her glass of lemonade back on the table. "Since I'm sure your task force did a good job of investigating Mason Construction, then you're well aware that my father is the one who ran things up until eight months ago, so he's the one who should receive all the credit. And yes, you're right, the success of Mason Construction speaks highly of his leadership skills. Dad was well liked and highly respected in this community."

Cameron Cody leaned back in his chair and Jocelyn thought that in addition to being successful, he was also extremely good looking, although she hadn't experienced any of the sizzle she'd felt when she first met Bas. And she hadn't felt that same jolt of current that had gone through her when their hands had made contact in a handshake as she'd felt with Bas. There had been no crackle or pop. She was a little daunted that it seemed her hyper-awareness of Bas was somewhat unique and at the moment unexplainable. Evidently there was some ingrained reason why Sebastian Steele could send heat shimmering through her with just a mere look or touch. She was clueless as to what it was.

She and Cameron were enjoying lunch at Kabuki, a popular Newton Grove restaurant that had a reputation for fine dining. Any time of any day, one would find it crowded with locals as well as tourists.

"You're not giving yourself enough credit, Ms. Mason," Cameron said smoothly, interrupting her thoughts. "But from all accounts, you've been doing a pretty good job since taking over things. The men who work for you respect you as well as admire your abilities and your knowledge of construction. To me that says a lot."

"Thank you." Once again she accepted his compliment, since from what she'd heard he didn't give them often. As she took another sip of her lemonade she got the feeling he didn't seem bothered that she had turned down his offer—an offer that had been rather generous. He had even gone so far as to assure her that the men who worked for her would remain employed with his corporation. She wondered if what she heard was true and that he had a telepathic sense when it came to good business deals. Did he think she would eventually change her mind?

Half an hour later she was walking through the front door of her home, hightailing it up the stairs to her bedroom to change clothes. She wanted to put in at least a few hours at the job site. After kicking off her shoes she wiggled out of her panty hose. While shimmying her skirt down her hips she noticed the red light blinking on the phone beside her bed. She quickly walked over to play the message.

"Jocelyn, this is Bas. I met with Marcella Jones this morning and explained the company's new policy regarding changes with her. She understood our position and has agreed to be surcharged for any additional changes she makes."

Jocelyn's mouth dropped open. Was he talking about the same Marcella Jones that everyone in Newton Grove knew? There's no way, she thought, quickly unbuttoning her blouse. If Bas had been able to get Marcella to cooperate, she couldn't help but wonder how. Then a thought hit her as she slipped into her jeans. No doubt Bas's good looks and perfect body had something to do with it; it was a known fact that even married, Marcella appreciated a nice piece of male flesh and had been involved in more than one extramarital affair. For some reason that thought didn't sit too well with Jocelyn.

She quickly pulled a T-shirt over her head and

before taking off down the stairs, she grabbed Bas's
jacket off the chair by her bedroom door, fully intend-
ing to return it to him today. As soon as she picked it
up the scent of him enslaved her, subduing her with
memories of the night before. For the rest of her life
she would remember that kiss, the way his tongue had
captured hers, sucked on it greedily, licked the
moisture from her mouth with a need that had nearly
pushed her over the edge and had sent intense desire
pounding in her head. Never in her life had she been
kissed that way. The very air surrounding them had
crackled with an intimacy she hadn't thought possible.

Just remembering the kiss, she felt overtaken by
something so erotic, so lustful and so plain feverish
that she had to hold her head down for a moment to
catch her breath and get her bearings. How could one
man have such a profound and sensuous impact on
a woman?

She didn't want to think what would have
happened if he had done more than kiss her. What if
he had gone beyond the kiss and had touched her intimately? What if his fingers had gotten involved
and had sneaked under her blouse to caress her
breasts, eased down to her stomach and beneath the
waistband of her jeans to slip inside her panties to
stroke the area between her legs, and then—

"Jocelyn, are you okay?"

Jocelyn jumped at the sound of her sister's voice and fought the urge to moan in total embarrassment. Leah was standing in the hallway looking at her with concern in her eyes. Barely able to breathe, Jocelyn made herself move quickly to the stairs. "Of course I'm all right. I was just thinking about something."

"Must have been something intense. For a moment you seemed to be in another world."

If only you knew, Jocelyn thought, taking the stairs two at a time. "I probably won't make it back in time for dinner tonight," she threw over her shoulder. "I want to use the computer at the office to check the Web for some arcade games we can lease for Founder's Day."

"No problem. I can always bring dinner to you."

Jocelyn turned, surprised by Leah's offer. Her sister had barely left the house since the funeral. Not only was she willing to venture out, but to the office, a place where she could very likely run into Reese. "Thanks. Are you sure you're up to doing that?"

Leah shrugged. "Yes. I still have no intention of ever telling Reese what happened, but I can't hide forever."

Jocelyn walked over to her sister to give her the hug she felt she needed. "No, you can't and I'm glad you finally realize that. But you know my feelings. I think that Reese deserves to know what happened."

Leah pulled back. "No, and you promised."

Jocelyn nodded. "And I plan to keep that promise, but I think it's something you need to think about, Leah. After you left, Reese was in a bad way. Do you know he hasn't seriously been involved with anyone since you?"

Leah's eyes widened in surprise. "No, I didn't know that."

Jocelyn smiled faintly. "And it wasn't from lack of interest on the women's parts, trust me. He refuses to let another woman get close enough to break his heart all over again."

Jocelyn watched a lone tear escape from Leah's eyes. She regretted having been so blunt but it wouldn't be fair for Leah not to know the depth of Reese's anger and pain.

Leah hung her head and said softly, "I never meant to hurt him, Jocelyn."

"Yes, I know, and now since you've told me everything, I understand. I just want you to be prepared for his attitude toward you if your paths ever cross. He's still hurt and rather bitter."

Leah tilted her head up and met Jocelyn's gaze. "Thanks for the warning."

"No problem," Jocelyn said, reaching out and touching Leah's arm. "And as far as dinner goes, don't worry about me. I ate a big lunch today."

She turned to leave but decided she needed to say something more to her sister. She turned back around. "I'm glad you're home, Leah, and more than anything, I don't want you hurting anymore."

She watched another tear fall from Leah's eyes. "Thanks, Jocelyn. That means a lot."

"Good."

Finally, Jocelyn left, and by the time she made it to her truck she felt good that she and Leah had crossed another hurdle together.

Chapter 5

"Why didn't you tell me about your meeting with
Cameron Cody?"

Jocelyn turned and lifted the safety glasses from
her eyes. All around was the loud noise of men busy
at work. Drills and saws were buzzing and hammers
and lumber were clashing, yet she'd been able to
hear Bas's question as if he'd been right on top of her
shouting in her ear when in fact he hadn't even raised
his voice. However, she could tell from the expression on his face that he wasn't a happy camper.

He leaned against a post with his hands shoved
into his pockets, his feet crossed at the ankles,

wearing faded jeans and a Carolina Panthers T-shirt. She wondered if the man had a patent on sexuality because whenever she saw him, no matter what he was wearing, he looked too damn good.

She swallowed back the bated breath that filled her throat. Having such a fierce attraction to a man was something she wasn't used to. He was beginning to be a pain in the butt in more ways than one.

"You know," she said, flipping her safety glasses back in place. "You've got a lot of nerve coming up behind a woman with a screwdriver in her hand."

Her gaze then traveled down the length of his body and deliberately froze on the area just below the belt. "Especially a woman who wouldn't mind giving new meaning to the term 'tightening up nuts' if she got angry enough."

He glared down at her. "Just answer my question, Jocelyn."

She glared back, not liking his attitude or his question. "I don't have to tell you everything that goes on with Mason Construction."

His step was quick and in two seconds, screwdriver or no screwdriver, he was standing directly in front of her. "Now that's where you're wrong. And since I prefer that the men didn't see us at odds with each other, I suggest we take this discussion elsewhere."

"Not interested," she said, already turning back around.

"Get interested. Let's go."

Before she could utter the next word, he grabbed her forearm and began tugging her along with him. She was grateful the men were too busy installing Marcella's granite countertops to give her or Bas the time of day. But still…

"Turn me loose," she warned him through clenched teeth. "Or you'll find out just how it feels to really get screwed."

That statement did the trick and he immediately dropped his hand from her arm. She was too ashamed to admit that her arm felt warm and tingly in the spot his fingers had been.

"We can use my car to go somewhere quiet."

His words reclaimed her attention and she stopped dead in her tracks. "Excuse me, but I'm not going anywhere with you. I have work to do."

His dark gaze clashed with hers. "Your work can wait. You owe me an explanation and I intend to get one. Have you forgotten that I'm also an owner in this company?" he asked tightly.

"A mere technicality. I'm buying you out just like I'm buying Leah out."

His lips twitched and it was hard to tell if it was due to anger or amusement. She got her answer when he said, "I never agreed to sell my part of this company to you. In fact I'm giving serious thought to keeping it. I just might go so far as to talk to your sister about purchasing her share and be willing to match generously any offer you make. Then, just think, Jocelyn, if that happens, we'll become equal partners."

Jocelyn tipped her head. She could feel the steam coming out of her ears. Her hand, still holding the screwdriver, itched. She'd never been a violent person but Bas was putting some mighty mean thoughts into her head right now. If he planned to become an equal partner with her, then he had another thought coming.

"Now that I have your attention," he said, looking down at her, "I think we need to go some place and talk."

Irritated, annoyed and angered beyond belief, Jocelyn expelled a deep breath. "Fine," she snapped. "We'll go somewhere to talk. But we'll take my truck."

Without giving him a chance to say anything, she turned and walked to where her truck was parked. And just as sure as she heard his footsteps right behind her, she knew that she had underestimated Sebastian Steele. It would never happen again.

"Just where the hell are you taking me?"

When Jocelyn brought the car to a traffic light, she tilted her head to one side and stared at Bas. Glared at him was more like it. "Not where I really want to take you, trust me."

Bas frowned. He'd never like smart-mouthed women.

"You wanted to talk so I'm taking you someplace where we can talk." She gave him a smile. It was polite and phony all rolled into one.

Bas's eyes narrowed. Not only did he not like smart-mouthed women, he liked even less women who thought they had the upper hand. "We don't have to go anywhere in particular," he decided to say, especially when he saw that damn screwdriver beside her on the seat. "We can talk just fine right now."

"Not while I'm driving, we can't," she said, rounding a corner on two wheels. And if that wasn't bad enough, she stepped on the gas to pass a speeding truck.

Bas had the good sense to reach out and spread his hands palms down against the dash. "Slow down. Are you trying to get us killed?"

She let out a short laugh that let him know she was still pretty pissed. "Now why would I want to do that?"

Yes, why indeed, Bas thought as he tested the shoulder harness of his seat belt. Okay, so maybe he should not have threatened to buy her sister's share—not that he had any intention of doing it anyway. There was one thing he and his brothers would not tolerate and that was anyone trying to come between them, whether it involved a business deal or otherwise. And there was no way he would have caused problems between Jocelyn and Leah by doing that same thing.

But he had wanted to make a point. When it came to him, she had better not assume anything. The right to sell or not to sell Mason Construction would have been her decision and he would not have taken it away from her. However, she needed to understand that there was such a thing as business respect.

"Okay, we're here."

He snapped out of his musings when the truck came to a stop. He swore as he hissed out a breath. Where in the world was he? When she nodded her head to the left, he saw the house through the clearing. It was a two-story brick structure with a double garage set in a bevy of tall oak trees that provided a lot of shade. And he could see the clear blue waters of a lake in the back.

"You know the people who live here?" he asked, admiring the structure and the land, which had to be at least ten acres.

"I'm the one who lives here," she muttered, opening the truck door and getting out.

He frowned as he watched her cross in front of the truck to get the mail out of a brick mailbox. She lived here? When she got back in the truck and thumbed through the letters, he stared at her for a moment then said, "I thought you lived in the house with Jim."

She glanced up at him. "I moved back home when Dad got sick, but I've been out on my own since I turned twenty-one. I lived in town in an apartment for a few years. I bought this place a year and half ago to stop Reese from burning it down."

Surprise glinted in the depths of Bas's eyes. "Reese was going to burn it down? Why?"

Jocelyn blew out a breath before tossing the envelopes on top of the dashboard. "This was Singleton land. At least this is the parcel that once belonged to Reese. He had always envisioned him and Leah living here together as man and wife, and without letting her know, he began building this house and was going to surprise her with it on her birthday. She left town before that. Afterward, Reese didn't have the heart to finish it."

Jocelyn paused a moment as if remembering that time. It was moments later before she continued. "At one point he hated this place, swore he would never finish it and even threatened to burn it to the ground. Dad and I talked him out of it. Told him if he didn't want it he should finish the work on it and sell it. And he did, to me."

Bas rolled down the window, suddenly needing air. Since he had never allowed a woman to cause him any pain, he could only imagine Reese's heartbreak. Hell, there wasn't a woman alive who could drive him to burn anything, not even a hot dog.

"Does your sister know about this house?" He had yet to meet Leah Mason but already from all accounts she sounded like a selfish person to turn her back on the love of a good man.

"No, she doesn't know *everything*."

Bas lifted a brow. "What doesn't she know?"

"She knows I bought the house from the Singletons but she doesn't know it had been meant for her." And now, after finding out the real reason Leah had left Newton Grove, in a way Jocelyn wished she wouldn't find out. That would only add to the guilt her sister was already carrying around.

Starting up the truck again, she said, "We didn't come here to talk about Reese and Leah."

"No, we didn't," he said, as she parked her truck in the driveway.

"I come here at least twice a week to get the mail and check on things." She tossed the words over her shoulder as she got out.

"When will you be moving back?" he asked, getting out the truck, as well.

"I hope in another week or so. I had planned to be back by now, but there's still a lot of Dad's stuff that Leah and I need to go through and I hadn't counted on Leah staying this long past the funeral, although I'm glad she has. And with the cost of gas, living in town has been convenient for me, although I miss the seclusion."

"You don't mind living this far from town alone?"

"Nope. I'm surrounded by so many people during the day that a secluded lifestyle pretty much suits me in the evenings and at night. Besides, Reese's brother and his wife live on the other side of the lake."

Bas didn't relish the thought of her living up here alone. His cousin Vanessa had bought a house in a rural section of Charlotte and it was awhile before he or his brothers got used to the idea. They still took turns checking on her every so often.

"Come on inside. I'll fix a pot of coffee and we can talk. I need to get clothes for the rest of the week anyway," she said as she started up the walkway.

Watching her stride toward the door was giving him a generous view of some very serious curves in her jeans, just like he'd gotten last night. But this time those curves were in motion and he could only stand and appreciate the sway of her hips. The sight was definitely holding him captive and he couldn't help but take the time to admire her. Not for the first time he thought that Jocelyn Mason was a very beautiful woman. Beautiful and tempting. And he quickly reminded himself that she was feisty. Too feisty for her own good...as well as for his.

Evidently noticing that he wasn't following meekly behind her, she stopped and turned around. "You got a problem?"

He recalled that was the same question he had tossed out at her last night. "No, I don't have a problem."

She nodded and began walking again. It was only then that he decided to follow. At least she had left that damn screwdriver in the car. For some reason he believed that if she got mad enough, she was a woman who made good on her threats.

Inside, Bas noted that the house was spacious, allowing a view of most of the rooms from the foyer, including a massive eat-in kitchen.

All the ceilings were vaulted and in the living room a brick fireplace was flanked by built-in book-cases. The furnishings were elegant, traditional, with the leather sofa, love seat, wingback chair and table lamps strategically placed facing the window to get a good view of the mountains. Every item in the room seemed to have a place and the beautiful splashes of earth-tone colors blended well with everything else, including the two oil paintings on the wall.

The dignified furnishings in this house, he noted, reflected a side of Jocelyn he hadn't seen a lot of yet—her prim and proper side. It showed a woman who had good taste and who liked beautiful things. Even the polished wood floors had character.

He reached out and traced a finger along a mahogany curio, noting the intricate detail and the fine craftsmanship. "Nice place and super-nice furniture," Bas said, glancing beyond the foyer and living room to the dining room where the furnishings there was just as elegant, traditional, sturdy.

"Thanks. Reese built all the furniture," Jocelyn said as she shoved her hands into the pockets of her jeans and leaned back against the wet bar that separated the dining room from the kitchen.

Bas's gaze shifted back to her, surprised. "He did?"

"Yes. He has a gift when it comes to using his hands on wood."

That, Bas thought, was an understatement. The man was definitely gifted. No wonder Jim had left him a tidy sum to start up his own business. He was wasting his talent at Mason Construction.

"This place was really too big for what I had in mind but like I said, I didn't want Reese to get rid of it," Jocelyn said, reclaiming Bas's attention.

The late-afternoon sunlight was shining through the huge kitchen window and the view of the lake from where they were standing was wonderful. But he thought the picture of Jocelyn standing in front of that window was even more so. She was a picture of refined elegance, just like her home.

"I can make us some coffee if—"

"No, I don't want anything," he said, interrupting what she was about to say. He thought it was safe to remember why they were there and not let other thoughts filter through his mind.

"I just want my question answered, Jocelyn. Why didn't you tell me about your meeting with Cody?" he asked, deciding to get down to business.

Jocelyn sighed as she stared at him. "The reason I didn't tell you was not because of some sinister plot on my part to keep you out of the loop about anything. I had honestly assumed you would accept my offer of a buy-out like Leah's doing. Why wouldn't I assume that? You and your brothers own a major corporation, the largest minority-owned one in North Carolina. You employ over a thousand people so I'm sure you're busy most of the time. To be quite frank with you, I'm surprised you're even here now. Not too many people would just up and drop everything and leave the running of a corporation even on a temporary basis to spend six to eight weeks supervising a construction company."

Bas nodded and shoved his own hands into the pockets of his jeans. "They would if the man who'd made the request was Jim Mason. Fourteen years ago I had left home with a chip on my shoulder and mad at the entire world. Your father helped me to turn my life around that summer and see things as they really were. If it hadn't been for him, no telling where I'd be today. I owe him a lot."

He decided it wasn't any of her business to know his other reason for coming—his health.

"Well, because I assumed what I did, I didn't

think twice about not including you in the meeting since I had every intention of telling Cody that the company wasn't for sale. He made me a good offer but I wasn't interested."

A question came into her head. "How did you know about my meeting with Cameron Cody?" She hadn't mentioned it to anyone, not even to Reese.

"Cameron told me, and yes, I know him. He was interested in one of my cousins a few years back. I was surprised when I ran into him in town. Because he's always on top of things, he was well aware I was one of the owners, but figured you were speaking in my and your sister's behalf when you turned down his offer."

Deliberately, Bas moved in front of her. "Okay, I'll accept the way you were thinking, but in the future don't assume anything, especially when it comes to me. I want to know about anything that involves this construction company, no matter how minor the detail. It's a matter of respecting me as one of the owners. Understood?"

Jocelyn frowned. She didn't like anyone talking to her as though she was a child, although he was right. She should have included him in her meeting with Cody. "Yes, I understand. Now it's time for you to understand something, as well."

"And just what might that be?"

"I'm not used to taking orders from any man

except my father. In the future if you have a request, it will pay you to make it nicely."

He lifted a brow. "Or else?"

"Or else it won't happen. I tried to explain to you that with this outfit everyone can't be a leader. Reese is the foreman and I respect his position, but when all is said and done, I'm still the boss."

"Um, sounds like you have an ego issue."

Annoyance rattled her at his words. "Sometimes in a man-dominated world women have to have one. But I don't think I have an ego issue. I just refuse to let anyone push me around." She stepped past him to walk over to the window. To Jocelyn's way of thinking Bas was standing too close. She could feel his heat. She could breathe in his scent. And both were doing crazy things to her mind as well as to her body. She was experiencing that tingling sensation in the pit of her stomach again.

"If you were one of my brothers I would challenge you to a game of basketball. Working off your frustrations can help."

She tipped her head to the side and looked at him. "I take it that whatever game you're involved in, you play to win."

"Yes, just about."

She couldn't help wondering how often he played any games. From what she'd seen in the past two days the man spent most of his time working. She was dying to know how he relieved stress.

"Okay, since you think I need to work off my frustrations, I have the perfect game."

He lifted his brow. "What?"

"Follow me."

She led him through the kitchen to the basement, and when he reached the bottom stair he stopped, grinned and let out a long whistle. The place resembled a sports bar with a huge plasma television screen on the wall, a wraparound bar with wooden stools as well as several pinball machines, a huge dartboard and a card table. And you couldn't miss the bold neon sign that read Jim's Place.

She must have read the question in his eyes because she said, "You know what a sports fanatic dad was, especially when it came to football. When I bought this house I decided to turn this room into a place where he and his cronies could hang out and enjoy whatever game they were into."

She chuckled. "On the weekends it became a regular hangout for him because there was always some game or another to watch on that huge television over there. It was nice seeing him and his friends have so much fun, and it felt good having him underfoot."

She swiped at the tears that suddenly appeared in her eyes and swore. "Damn, but I'm going to miss him."

Bas was across the room in a flash and gently pulled Jocelyn into his arms. "Hey, it's going to be okay. And it's all right to miss him. He was a good man and from what I can tell you were a good daughter. He had to have been proud of this place that you provided here for him, his own entertainment spot. That was pretty nice of you considering I bet Jim and his buddies could get rather loud at times," he said flicking her a teasing smile.

She chuckled. "If only you knew. I would be upstairs in bed reading with my ear plugs in. Still, it felt good knowing he was having a good time. They will be memories I will cherish forever, Bas."

"And you should. My parents retired a few years ago to move to Florida and left me and my brothers in charge. My first thought was good riddance, we wouldn't have to put up with Dad constantly checking our decisions or Mom forcing us to Sunday dinner. But they hadn't been gone two weeks and we were all missing them like crazy. We even thought about calling and telling them to move back. But then we decided it would have been selfish on our part. It was their time to enjoy life."

He squeezed her hand in assurance. "And from what I can see, you did that, Jocelyn. You gave Jim a chance to enjoy life."

"Everyone should," she said, moving around him

to cross the room when she began feeling hot and tingly again. She stopped when she came to one of the pinball machines and turned around.

Her breath caught in her throat. He was looking at her the same way he'd been looking at her right before he had kissed her last night…and that wasn't good. She tried getting her bearings and said, "So, are you ready to play a game?"

He leaned against the bar and she watched his eyes darken. "And just what sort of game do you have in mind?"

Evidently not the one you're thinking about, she wanted to say. She might not have a lot of experience with men but she definitely could recognize one with heat in his eyes. "How about a game of pinball?"

He chuckled. "Pinball?"

"Yes. Don't you know how to play?"

"Sure, I do."

"Okay then, but I understand if you think you're not up to holding your own against me and—"

"Not up to holding my own?"

"Yes."

Still smiling, Bas crossed the room to where she stood. He'd planned to spend most of the evening at Mason Construction, going through some more files and working way past midnight again. But he refused to let Jocelyn think she could best him at a pinball machine. And this particular baby just happened to be a Stern Nascar. "Ms. Mason, you're about to meet the king of pinball."

She looked at him and grinned. "You think so?"

"I know so."

Jocelyn figured now was not the time to let him know that last year she had won the local pinball competition. She began rolling up her sleeve and grinned at him. "Okay, Steele, you're on."

Chapter 6

"Are you always into keeping secrets, Jocelyn?" Bas asked frowning, after they had finished their last game and were walking back up the steps from the basement. "You should have told me upfront that you were a pinball champion."

Jocelyn chuckled. "Why? And take all the fun out of winning?"

When they reached the landing he said, "Hey, champion or no champion, you only won because I wasn't playing my best since I didn't think I had to. I assumed this was an easy win."

She crossed her arms beneath her breasts and

stared at him. "What were you saying earlier about *assuming* anything?"

Bas hooked a thumb into his jeans. "That was different."

She smiled. "Of course you would say that." She then checked her watch. "Give me a second to grab some clothes and I'll be ready to go back to town," she said turning toward her bedroom.

"Take your time. I need privacy to lick my wounds anyway."

She paused in the archway between the hall and her bedroom. "Too bad you're a sore loser."

"I'm not."

"You are, too. Admit it."

"Okay, I like to win."

"So do I."

"You know I'm going to want a rematch."

"We'll see." And with that said, she disappeared inside her bedroom.

Bas couldn't stop the chuckle that escaped his lips. Damn, he had spent the last two hours racking up over a billion points and still had lost to a female hotshot. The number of bonus points she'd gotten was downright sickening.

He shook his head, not believing he had actually taken time away from work to play a damn game of pinball. It had been the weirdest thing how his adrenaline had gotten pumped up, practically the same way it did whenever he played basketball against his brothers. He hadn't even thought about the files he had planned to go over at the office. The only thing he had thought about was whipping Jocelyn's butt big-time.

And what a butt it was. It didn't take much to remember her in front of the pinball machine, her stance sexy and stimulating as hell, and her display of excitement each and every time she deployed a ball. Just being able to ogle her undetected had been worth the loss. Once again he couldn't help but think about the too-serious curves on her body and what they did to a pair of jeans and a top. Each time her butt had moved, he'd found it almost impossible to sit still, stand still or to stop a certain part of him from getting hard.

He had played enough pinball to know it was a mental game and if you weren't focused there was no chance in hell you could win. Of course he hadn't been focused. He hadn't even used a lot of the skilled flipper work he often used when he played against his brothers.

It was difficult to concentrate when you were playing against a woman whose perfume smelled of seduction and whose body made you think of a different kind of scoring. He'd known that whenever her tongue licked her lips she was setting up her shots to score big. And he had wanted to capture that same tongue with his.

"I'm all set."

He turned at the sound of her voice and crossed the room to relieve her of the load of clothes she carried.

Their hands touched and an electric current quickly flowed through their bodies. Silence hung between them for a long moment until she finally said, "Thanks."

"Don't mention it."

"We'd better go."

He sighed deeply. "Yes, I think we'd better."

By the time Jocelyn had locked up and they had walked back out to her truck, Bas wanted to punch something. The desire to kiss her had been so strong he'd felt his self-control slipping, and for the first time in a long time he hadn't wanted to do anything to regain it.

He didn't have to be a rocket scientist to know that if he didn't pull himself together he was headed for big trouble.

"So, what're your plans for dinner?"

The truck had come to a stop at a traffic light and Jocelyn glanced over at Bas. "I don't have any. Why?"

"After playing that game with you, I've worked up an appetite and thought we could stop and grab something to eat."

Jocelyn laughed. "I couldn't help noticing how much you got into the game. You're a good player."

"Yet you won."

"Yeah, but to give you credit I have to admit you played well. One of the keys to winning pinball is to concentrate on what shots are going to give you the biggest points."

He decided not to tell her the real reason he'd lost was because he'd been concentrating on her more than the game. "I was serious when I said I wanted a rematch," he said.

"I'm sure you were, and I don't mind accommodating you if you can handle another loss."

He laughed. "Kind of confident, aren't you?"

She smiled. "When playing pinball one has to be."

The sun had gone down and dusk was settling in, but even with the dim light in the truck's cab, Bas could see Jocelyn's features clearly, and a funny feeling flowed all through him. He turned to look out the window, thinking it was safer to do so. His attraction to her wasn't good at all. In fact it was bad news.

"So what are your plans?"

Jocelyn's question intruded into his thoughts and he glanced over at her. "Not sure, but I need something to eat." And nothing fried, he further thought, remembering Dr. Nelson's words as well as the promise he'd made to his sister-in-law. He'd gone a week without any fried chicken and it was about to kill him. Each time he passed a KFC he had to keep his control in check and not go in and order the dark-meat special.

"That place up there serves good food," she said, pointing to a restaurant just ahead.

"They have chicken?"

"Yes."

"Baked?"

"Yes, and it's pretty good. It's nice to meet a man who doesn't have to eat fried chicken. All that grease isn't good for you."

He decided not to tell her that all that grease was what he wanted, but he'd been sentenced to a life without it for a while. "Will you stop and have dinner with me?"

When she came to another traffic light, she settled her gaze on his, and he knew she was trying to make her mind up about whether she would join him for dinner. "Come on, you've got to eat some time," he coaxed.

Another smile touched her lips. "I had a big lunch, but I do know for a fact that restaurant makes a dynamite salad."

He couldn't imagine anyone just having a salad for a meal, but he said anyway, "Okay, then what are we waiting for?"

She eased the truck into the turning lane and

laughed. "Not one single thing. Besides, I'm curious as to how you got Marcella Jones to go along with those surcharges."

For a Tuesday night the place was crowded, but fortunately, enough waitresses were working the tables and within a few minutes Jocelyn and Bas had been seated.

"Um, I can just smell the fried chicken," Bas said, inhaling the air and licking his lips.

Jocelyn raised a brow. "I thought you were getting baked."

"I am." He took a sip of coffee before picking up his menu.

"So how did you do it?" Jocelyn asked, glancing over her own menu. She wondered why she was bothering to look at it since she knew exactly what she wanted. But then looking at the menu meant she didn't have to look at Bas, because looking at Bas made her insides sizzle. Something about the restaurant's lighting made him that much more eye-droppingly handsome. She couldn't help noticing that the waitresses were definitely checking him out.

"How did I do what?"

His question reeled in her thoughts. "Get Marcella to cooperate."

Blowing out a breath he said, "Trust me, it wasn't easy."

"So how did you do it?" she asked again.

Bas decided it was best Jocelyn didn't know all the gory details. Just like Sadie, Marcella had remembered him from those summers long ago. She was brazen as hell and had actually told him how turned on she used to get seeing him shirtless, and she more than hinted that she would like to see him without his shirt again, or his pants.

He had remained professional and had told her in a nice way he wasn't interested in undressing for her and that their only business was the building of her house. She hadn't appreciated her sexual advances being turned down and had tried being difficult. He had refused to let her get on his last nerve, and had finally said since the two of them couldn't see eye to eye he would deal with her husband. Evidently, she'd gotten concerned that Bas would mention her less than estimable behavior to Mr. Jones, and decided to cooperate.

"At first she wasn't having any of what I said, so I told her I would discuss the situation with her husband. In the end, let's just say Marcella Jones and I decided it was best to keep her husband out of it."

Jocelyn's lips quirked. "She came on to you, didn't she?"

He lifted a brow. "Why would you think that?"

Jocelyn chuckled. "Because I know Marcella. Over the years I've heard the rumors. She came on to Reese when we were building her first house and he had to put her in her place. Unfortunately for her it was during the time Reese had sworn off all women. We were surprised she came to us to build another house for her. Rumor has it that she likes them young."

Bas took another sip of coffee. "She can't be that old."

"Try forty-five."

Bas blinked at her. "You're kidding."

"Nope. I admit she wears her age well. Most people take her to be ten years younger at least."

At that moment the waitress, who was all but drooling while looking at Bas, came back to take their orders. "I'll have a chef's salad," Jocelyn said, closing the menu.

The young woman nodded. She then turned her complete attention to Bas. Jocelyn couldn't help noticing that the waitress had undone the top button of her uniform and was now showing a lot of cleavage. And it was plain to see she was wearing a push-up bra.

"And what will you have?" the waitress asked Bas, all but purring the words.

Jocelyn had always thought that jealousy was a complete waste of time and energy, but watching the woman in action was almost too much. She glanced over at Bas while he gave his order. He either didn't see how the waitress was coming on to him or he was choosing to ignore it.

Feeling a little agitated, Jocelyn was about to excuse herself to go to the ladies' room when Bas reached over, squeezed her hand and said, after looking at the waitress's name tag, "And if you don't mind, Stacy, my fiancée and I would like to be served as soon as the cook can get it ready. We're in a hurry to get home."

Jocelyn saw the disappointment in the woman's eyes before she nodded and left. Jocelyn shook her head and slowly pulled her hand from Bas's. She didn't want to think how good his hand felt encompassing hers.

"That woman had some nerve coming on to you that way with me sitting here. For all she knew I could have been your wife."

Bas smiled. "She probably thought you weren't since you aren't wearing a ring."

Jocelyn frowned. "That shouldn't mean anything. The mere fact that I'm here with you should have garnered respect."

"Yes, it should have."

"You should not have had to pretend anything was going on between us."

"No, I should not have."

Jocelyn glared. The way he was agreeing with everything she said irked her. "I'm not amused, Bas."

His expression turned genuinely serious. "Neither am I, Jocelyn. We can always leave if she offended you. And if you want to stay we can request another waitress."

She shook her head. Another waitress would only drool like the last one had. In the woman's defense, though, she had to admit that cleft in Bas's chin was patently masculine and completed the total sexy package. Not that she'd say it aloud. "No, I'm fine. It just bothers me how brazen some women are. I would never be that bold."

And a part of Bas appreciated that she wouldn't. He couldn't imagine Jocelyn ever handling herself inappropriately. However, on the other hand, she could put you in your place if she felt the need.

"I think you're going to enjoy your baked chicken," she said a few minutes later.

Bas glanced over at the table next to theirs where a man had ordered fried chicken and seemed to be enjoying it. Bas felt his stomach whine. Sighing deeply, he said, "I really hope so."

Bas had to admit his food was delicious. He had been careful while ordering to stay away from the items on the menu that Kylie had told him were a no-no. He couldn't help but smile, thinking about how his sister-in-law had encased herself in his and his brothers' lives.

Once she had found out that he needed to make a change in his eating habits, she had taken it upon herself to educate him on the proper food choices. It was a good thing he was here in Newton Grove. Had he remained in Charlotte he would be starving on some strict menu Kylie thought best for him.

"You're smiling. Does that mean you think the food tastes good?" Jocelyn asked.

He glanced up and the smile on his lips widened. "Yes, it tastes good, but that's not why I'm smiling. I was thinking about my sister-in-law."

"Your sister-in-law?"

"Yes. Kylie," he said, tossing his napkin down and leaning back in his chair. "She's a very nice person and the best thing to ever happen to my brother in a long time. They've only been married eight months."

"Which brother is this? You mentioned you had three." From Bas's smile Jocelyn could tell that he and his brothers shared a close relationship.

"Kylie's married to Chance, the oldest at thirty-seven. Then there are Morgan and Donovan. Chance is the only one of us who's ever been married. He was a widower for seven years and has a sixteen-year-old son named Marcus."

Bas chuckled. "In fact, Marcus and Kylie's

daughter, Tiffany, who is fifteen, are the reason Chance and Kylie are together."

Jocelyn wiped her mouth with a napkin before asking. "How is that?

"By playing cupid."

For the next twenty minutes Bas told Jocelyn how Marcus and Tiffany had felt that neither of their strict parents had a life and had decided to do something about it by orchestrating a plan to shift their parents' attention off them and onto each other.

Instead of using the napkin to wipe at her mouth, Jocelyn began dabbing at her eyes while laughing. She'd found the teens' escapades totally hilarious. "Well, evidently their plan worked."

Bas chuckled. "Yes, it did. Quite successfully." He took advantage of the break in conversation to question why he was here, sharing dinner with Jocelyn, instead of back at the office going through files. Although he wanted to think that this entire afternoon had been a total waste of good time, he couldn't. He had to admit that he enjoyed the time he had spent with Jocelyn, although it had started out pretty damn rocky.

He'd gotten a kick out of playing pinball with her even when she was slaughtering him in points, and dinner had been rather nice, as well. He felt comfortable talking to her, sharing tidbits about his family. The last woman he'd taken out had been Cassandra and they'd gone to an exclusive restaurant. She had spent the entire evening criticizing the outfits other women were wearing. To hear her talk, she was the only fashion plate in the place.

"You mentioned that Cameron Cody was interested in one of your cousins."

Bas studied the dark liquid in his glass and grinned. After dinner they had ordered scrumptious cheesecake and a glass of delicious dessert wine to go along with it. "Yes, and I have a feeling he still is. I met Cameron a few years ago when he tried to take over the Steele Corporation."

Jocelyn lifted a brow, not sure she had heard him correctly. "Cody tried forcing a takeover of your company?"

"Yes, and he would have been successful if my brothers and three cousins and I hadn't stuck together, which proved what a unified force we were. The Steele Corporation was formed over twenty-five years ago by my father and my Uncle Harold. It was always understood that I and my three brothers, as well as Uncle Harold's three daughters—Vanessa, Taylor and Cheyenne—would one day inherit the company. All of us are working there except for Taylor and Cheyenne. They decided to pursue careers outside of the corporation, although they sit on the board. Uncle Harold passed away ten years ago and my father retired five years after that, leaving Chance as CEO."

He took another sip of his wine before continuing. "As soon as word got out about my father's retirement, several corporate marauders tried to force a takeover. Cameron's company was just one of them."

Jocelyn took a sip of her own wine. "But when you mentioned him earlier I got the impression the two of you are friends."

Bas smiled and Jocelyn noticed each time he did so his dimples appeared and the cleft in his chin seemed even more profound. "We are. My brothers and I couldn't help but admire Cameron's accomplishments and give him the respect he's due. He earned everything he has, and he's built his empire by working hard. Anything he got he deserved. He is a hard man but fair. Once he saw that his attempt to take us over was futile, he pulled out and set his sights on another Steele—my cousin Vanessa. She heads our PR department. My brothers and I got over what Cameron tried to do and eventually became friends with him. However, Vanessa never could and as much as Cameron tried, he couldn't break through the barriers she had erected."

A half hour later, Jocelyn was returning Bas to the job site so he could get his car. It was almost ten o'clock. "You aren't thinking about going over to the office, are you?" she asked when she brought her truck to a stop next to his parked car.

He shook his head and chuckled. "No, not tonight.

I think I'll go home and come up with a game plan to beat you at pinball the next go-round."

She returned his chuckle. "Come up with any game plan you want. The outcome will still be the same."

"We'll see."

She looked at him and said smartly, "Yes, we *will* see."

More than anything Bas wanted to kiss her. He still had memories of their last kiss, but he wanted to replace them with new memories. "Maybe," he said, leaning a little closer to her across the truck's bench seats, "we should consider a wager."

"A wager?" she asked, her voice soft, low.

"Yes."

"Sorry, but I don't make bets."

"But what if it's for something you might like?" he asked, lifting his hand to cup her cheek and feeling glad that she didn't pull back.

"Like what?"

"You tell me. What is it you want?" he asked, leaning even closer and hearing her suck in a deep breath.

"How about letting me buy you out so you can leave here by the weekend?"

He shook his head and released an easy chuckle. "Sorry, can't do that. Think of something else."

"What if I don't want anything else?"

"Then you need to think harder." His hand left her cheek and moved to the back of her neck.

"Can't think harder."

"Why not?"

"Because when you're this close to me, you make it impossible to think at all."

"Aw hell, Jocelyn." The words slipped from between Bas's lips just seconds before he captured her mouth with his. The moment their lips touched he remembered how good she had tasted the last time and was getting his fill of how good she was tasting now. That intangible chemistry they had been dealing with from the first day was back full force. If truth be known, it had never left. It was even more potent, compelling and intoxicating. That passionate moan she was making wasn't helping matters one bit. But what really made him lose it was when she laid a hand on his thigh to keep her balance. Whether she realized it or not—and he believed she didn't— her hand was too damn close to a part of him that was aching for her.

He deepened the kiss, their tongues mating, and he thought she was better than the dessert he'd had at dinner. They continued to kiss and for a while he thought he could spend the rest of the night doing just this. But he knew the last thing they should be doing was sitting in a parked truck at a vacant job site kissing, so he fought to regain control and slowly, with all the reluctance in the world, pulled back.

In the semi-darkened cab he saw her moist lips tremble, and he was tempted to lean forward and take them with his again. But he couldn't do that. He needed to go somewhere to clear his head and figure out what there was about Jocelyn Mason that made him want to take her somewhere and make love to her. All night and all day.

And that wasn't a good thought.

He sighed deeply. "I'd better go."

"All right," she said brushing her hair from her face and resnapping her seat belt. "I had fun with you today, Bas. You're not such a bad guy."

He smiled over at her. "Friends, then?"

She chuckled. "I wouldn't go that far. I'm not Cameron Cody. I don't make friends easily with the enemy."

He lifted a brow. "And you see me as the enemy?"

His question hung over them for a few minutes before she said, "I don't know how I see you," she said honestly. "I don't want you here and now you're beginning to complicate things."

"Why? Because of a few kisses?"

"Yes, because of a few kisses." *Not to mention all that heat that is surging between my thighs right now.*

"How about a truce?" he interrupted her thoughts by asking.

"Another one?"

He chuckled. "They can only get better."

That was exactly what she was afraid of.

"So what do you say? Truce?" he asked again, sticking his hand out.

She took it and immediately felt the heat between her legs get hotter. "Okay, another truce."

At that moment Jocelyn hoped she hadn't agreed to something she would later regret.

Chapter 7

Jocelyn felt the tap on her shoulder and slowly turned around to find Leah smiling at her. "Here. You look like you need this."

"I do and thanks." Jocelyn smiled and accepted the cup of steaming coffee and took a sip. Yes, she really did need it and nobody could make coffee like Leah. That was another thing she had missed when her sister had left. Sighing deeply, she turned back to look out the kitchen window.

"I heard you pacing the floor last night."

Jocelyn turned again and met Leah's gaze. "You did?"

"Yes." Leah walked across the kitchen to lean against the counter. "I know I agreed to sell you my part of Mason Construction, but is something going on that I should know about?"

Jocelyn frowned. "Something like what?"

Leah shrugged. "Um, I don't know. Anything. You paced the floor for a good thirty minutes or more."

Jocelyn knew it was more, although she hadn't been keeping time. "No, nothing is going on," she said, and then shifted from Leah's curious gaze to glance back out the window again.

She hadn't been able to sleep because thoughts of Sebastian Steele kept invading her mind. For the second time she had allowed him to kiss her, and there were things about him that she didn't know.

Last night at dinner he had talked freely about his brothers and cousins, but he hadn't mentioned anything about himself. In fact, he seemed very careful not to do so. She was pretty convinced he wasn't married and never had been, since he'd mentioned his brother Chance had been the only sibling who'd ever tied the knot. But what about a girlfriend or even worse, a fiancée? Men who looked like Bas usually weren't unattached, at least not for long.

"Well, I'm going to take your word that everything is fine," Leah said, glancing down at her watch. "I need to leave or I'm going to be late."

Jocelyn quickly turned around. "You're going somewhere?" she asked, noticing for the first time her sister was wearing slacks and a blouse and had her purse strapped to her shoulder.

Leah smiled. "Yes, don't you remember? I told you last night when you came in that I made an appointment at Kate's Beauty Salon."

Jocelyn nodded. Oh, yes, she remembered now. Leah *had* mentioned it but at the time Jocelyn's mind had been overtaken with memories of Bas's kiss. "That's right you did. How are you getting it styled?"

Leah chuckled. "I told you that, too. I even showed you the model in the picture I tore out of a magazine. You must have really been out of it last night." She tipped her head to the side to study Jocelyn. "Is Marcella Jones still driving all of you nuts?"

"No, it's not Marcella."

"Then it must be Sebastian Steele."

Hearing her sister say Bas's name had Jocelyn's heart pounding. "Why would you think that?"

"Because I got the impression a few days ago that he was getting on your nerves and you hadn't accepted him being here, not to mention his role with Mason Construction. I know how much you detest anyone looking over your shoulder. Just remember he's here for a good reason and when he leaves you probably won't ever hear from him again."

Jocelyn noted that Leah was smiling brightly, as if what she'd said should cheer Jocelyn up, yet it didn't. For some reason the thought of Bas leaving anytime soon was something Jocelyn didn't want to think about, although she had asked him to do that very thing last night.

"Maybe you're right."

"More than likely I am," Leah said as if to assure her. "I checked out the Steele Corporation on the Internet yesterday. Sebastian Steele is a pretty wealthy guy who is used to a big city like Charlotte. There's nothing to keep him here. He's probably itching to get back to the lifestyle he left behind."

A half hour later, after Leah had left, Jocelyn was in her room getting dressed. Instead of reporting to the job site, she had a meeting scheduled with her Founder's Day Celebration committee, especially those members working closely with her on the ball. The governor had accepted an invitation and Jocelyn wanted to make sure all their plans were on target.

She shifted her thoughts to the conversation she'd had earlier with Leah. Jocelyn herself had checked out that same Web site and Leah was right. A man of Bas's status would have no reason to hang around Newton Grove any longer than necessary, not that she wanted him to hang around, mind you. But there had been something about them sharing dinner that wouldn't leave her alone.

Maybe it was the way he tipped his head whenever she was talking to let her know she had his absolute attention. Or it might have been the slow and methodical way he sipped his wine that had heat thrumming through her body each time she watched the liquid pass down his throat. Or maybe, just maybe, it had been the toe-curling kiss she couldn't seem to forget. Each time his tongue got hold of hers it was as if he was branding it while she went soaring into mind-blowing passion.

Jocelyn groaned. She'd never let any man get to her the way Bas was doing. But then she had to reconcile herself to the fact that there was a first time for everything.

Across town someone was having a similar rough morning. Bas frowned when he looked down at the bowl Ms. Sadie had placed in front of him. Oatmeal?

He had been deprived of a good night's sleep and he'd be damned if he'd be deprived of a good breakfast, as well. Where were the bacon, sausage, grits, eggs and toast whose aroma had awakened him that morning?

He glanced up and found Sadie Robinson looking at him with a smug smile. She had the nerve to say, "And if you drop by for lunch I'll prepare you a luscious fruit salad."

His frown deepened. When he thought of fruit he didn't think of luscious. When he thought of Jocelyn he thought of luscious, which was one of the reasons he hadn't slept well.

But that didn't explain why he was only getting oatmeal for breakfast and fruit for lunch. He was more than certain Ms. Sadie hadn't run out of food, since yesterday he'd noticed on his way out that she tended to cook a rather large quantity of everything. So what was going on?

Not taking his gaze off her, he asked in as calm a voice as he could, "Is there something going on that I should know about?"

Sadie never took her eyes off Bas either when she responded in a not-so-innocent voice, "Why would you think that?"

Ordinarily, Bas might let the matter go, eat the damn oatmeal and be merry about it. But not this morning after having had dream after dream of a woman he'd best leave alone. He might never make love to her in reality but in his fantasies he could still see the heated look in the depths of her dark-brown eyes each and every time he—

"Besides, oatmeal is good for you."

Sadie's words interrupted his thoughts. A frustrated gush of air shot from his lungs and he leaned back in his chair and stared at the older woman with a look that usually told his brothers and cousins to back off. Evidently she didn't get the message because she continued talking.

"It's a good thing I noticed your medication while cleaning your room yesterday or I would never have known you were on a restricted diet. And now that I know I—"

"You were in my room yesterday?" he interrupted her, leaning forward in the chair and piercing her with an even deeper look.

"How else do you think it got clean?"

Bas's scowl deepened but it didn't seem to affect Sadie Robinson any. "So you snooped into my things?" he asked incredulously.

She waved her hand in the air. "Of course not. The pill bottle was right there on the counter in the bathroom. I had to pick it up and move it to clean off the area. Of course, when I did I couldn't help but notice you're taking the same medication my Albert used to take."

Her Albert? Bas hadn't realized she was married. "And where is *your Albert*?"

"Dead."

Out of respect, he bit back the word *damn* as he rubbed a hand down his face. That was all he needed to know. Her Albert who used to take the same medication he took was dead. Although Bas wished he could move on without asking the next question, something inside him made him inquire anyway.

"And how did he die?"

"He had high blood pressure and although the medication helped, he refused to give up some of his favorite foods that were killing him. And knowing what happened to Albert, I can't in good conscience allow the same thing to happen to you."

Bas lifted a brow, sure he'd heard her wrong. "Excuse me?"

She crossed her arms over her chest. "I said I won't allow the same thing to happen to you. My Albert only thought of himself. He should have cared enough to want to live longer so he could be here with me while we spent our retirement years together. But he didn't take care of himself and now he's gone. We were married almost fifty years and had four beautiful children and he didn't live long enough to be around for the first great-grand. I tried to tell him to eat healthy. I even offered to prepare him all the foods that were better for him. But he refused to give up that steak twice a week, as well as the potatoes, the bread and let's not talk about the desserts."

No, Bas didn't want to talk about the desserts. He didn't want to talk about food period. "But I'm not your husband, Ms. Sadie," he decided it was time to point out.

"No, but some day you'll be somebody's husband if you live long enough. You're young, too young to be worried about some nasty ailment like high blood pressure, which can lead to other problems like heart disease. It's best that you get a handle on things now before it's too late. And while you're living here I intend to help you. I owe it to my Albert and your mother to do so."

Bas shook his head in frustration. "But you don't know my mother."

"Doesn't matter. We're all members of the 'Mothers Club' and I know wherever she is, she'll thank me for trying to save her son from an early grave."

Bas sighed deeply, recognizing the stubborn glint in the woman's eyes. It was the same glint he'd seen in his own mother's eyes several times, and the one he had seen in Kylie's the day she had confronted him after finding out about his medical issues. Ms. Sadie was right. Once a mother, always a mother. All mothers shared a bond to make their kids' lives miserable.

Bas decided to use another approach. "Ms. Sadie, don't you think getting involved in my medical business is carrying things a little too far? I'm just a resident here for a while. I'm a grown man—thirty-five. Shouldn't my eating habits be my decision to make?"

"Yes."

Bas nodded, glad they were finally getting somewhere. "And don't you think you've crossed the line by serving me oatmeal instead of the breakfast you gave to everyone else this morning?"

He watched as the older woman pushed a curly lock of gray hair away from her face and in that instant he saw it—the look of stark worry in her eyes. She actually thought his fate could be sealed like her Albert's if he didn't eat differently. Aw hell. All he needed was the old woman worrying to death about him. And although she had agreed that what he ate was his business, he knew as far as she was concerned, to feed him the high-calorie foods he liked would be like signing his death warrant.

Bas knew there was only one thing he could do and that would be to find another place to stay as soon as he could. He refused to hang around Newton Grove for the next three months and live under the same roof with an older version of Kylie Hagan Steele.

It just so happened he had run across a place for sale the day he'd been out riding around with Reese. It was a quaint little cabin just outside of town on a small lake in the mountains. If nothing else it would be a nice piece of investment property. He would see a realtor about it first thing tomorrow.

He met Ms. Sadie's gaze. "Fine," he said. "I'll eat the oatmeal every morning if it makes you happy." *Just until I get that cabin,* he decided not to add.

Her worried look brightened into a smile. "Thank

you and it will. And when you live to your late seventies with kids, grands and great-grands like me, you'll be grateful that someone cared enough about you to make sure you stuck to a proper diet."

"Not a chance," Bas muttered under his breath as he scooted back to the table to eat his oatmeal.

Leah smiled as she looked at herself in the oval mirror she held in her hand. "I think even after all these years no one can take care of a woman's head like you can, Kate."

The older woman chuckled and waved her hand as if refusing to accept the flattering comment. "Doing your hair has always been easy. I'm glad you didn't put all that crazy dye in it while living out in Los Angeles. That would have damaged it for sure. Your hair is just as thick and healthy as it's always been."

Leah smiled at the compliment. "Thanks." Kate had been doing her hair ever since Leah was a teenager and her dad had agreed to let her get a perm. Kate was right, Leah's hair had always been thick and healthy, but what Kate had been too nice to add was that it had also been unmanageable. While Jocelyn could get by with going to the hair salon every two weeks, Kate was sentenced to see Leah on a weekly basis.

Leah couldn't help but remember those times. Jocelyn had been close to their father and she had been close to their mother. She'd died when Leah had been only twelve, and all Leah could remember was how empty she'd felt. Jocelyn had always been Daddy's girl and hadn't experienced the same sense of loss as Leah had. From the day they'd placed her mother in the ground, Leah couldn't wait to move away from a town filled with loneliness for her without the mother she had adored.

"I was sorry to hear about your dad, Leah. Everyone around here was. He was a good man."

Leah nodded. She hadn't realized just what a good man he was until she'd found herself alone, hurt and out in California on her own. More than once she'd come close to picking up the phone and telling him what had happened to her and why she'd left the way she had. But shame had kept her from doing so.

Her only saving grace was actually someone with the name of Grace. How she had ended up on the woman's doorstep one night, she still wasn't sure. All she knew was that she was convinced she'd heard footsteps behind her while walking home alone from the restaurant where she'd worked. Remembering what had happened to her before, she had gone almost stone-crazy and had run to the first house she'd come to and begged for help.

Help had come in the way of an older woman, no bigger than a mite, who had offered her safety.

Grace Thorpe had been a godsend. After making sure Leah was safe, she'd offered her food to eat and a place to stay, much better than the dump where she'd been living.

Grace's two sons had threatened to move their mother in with them and their wives on a rotating basis, not wanting the old woman to live alone anymore. What Grace had needed was a companion, someone to be there with her during the day and to do the grocery shopping and drive Grace to church on Sundays. Since Leah worked at the restaurant at night, she grabbed the opportunity.

Half an hour later after leaving the hair salon, Leah was strolling through downtown Newton Grove, checking out the various shops and noticing what changes the town had made over the years. After living in the hustle and bustle of L.A. for five years, she appreciated the solitude and quiet a place like Newton Grove offered. She'd never realized how much she missed living in this town until now.

Tossing her hair out of her eyes, she kept walking, remembering a place close by that used to sell breakfast and wondering if it was still open. She had gotten up early and had started a pot of coffee but hadn't made breakfast for herself, or her sister, who rarely took the time for breakfast.

Jocelyn.

Leah couldn't help but wonder what was going on

with her sister. There was never a time she didn't think her older sister was in control and made things happen just the way she wanted. But now, at twenty-three, Leah was seeing things through different eyes, more appreciative and caring eyes, and she hoped that whatever had caused Jocelyn to walk the floor last night would go away.

Leah passed in front of a store window and stopped. Then she noticed what had grabbed her attention. It was a baby store with a number of items on display. She pulled her jacket closer around her and not for the first time she remembered the dream she'd had to let go of years ago.

She would never have the baby she always wanted. A little one she could bounce on her knee, sing lullabies to and sprinkle with the scent of baby powder. She had dreamed about this child of hers for so long and how he would look up at her with dark-brown eyes and the same smile that had gone straight to her heart—like his father's had done six years ago. There was nothing that could even make her think of staying in Newton Grove until she had met Reese the summer before her senior year of high school.

Love and caring hadn't meant a damn thing to her until then. The only thing she wanted to do was hurry up and graduate and haul ass, go as far west and away from Tennessee as a plane ticket could take her.

Then, in a slow, methodical process Reese had broken down her defenses. He had done something no one else had been able to do—he'd understood her loss. He had listened when she had wanted to talk about her mother. He had understood her pain and sense of loss because he had experienced those same things himself when he'd lost his father at sixteen. With patience, care and understanding, he had made her fall in love with him in a way that was so complete that she hadn't thought of leaving town. The only thing she had wanted to do was to hang around, marry him and have his babies.

But now that was a dream that would never come true. Although there was no physical reason why she couldn't have a child, she would never be able to let a man touch her that way. At one point she had thought about artificial insemination, but a lot of things prevented that. First, she didn't have the money and her insurance would not cover such a procedure. Second, she would still have to take off her clothes for the procedure, and she couldn't do that in front of anyone. Third, the thought of carrying a baby from someone she didn't know was a turn-off for her. The only man's baby she'd ever dreamed of having was Reese's.

Feeling a knot settling in her throat, she wiped a hand across her face, swiping at the tears that she couldn't stop from flowing down her cheeks. Life was cruel, but considering all the hard times she had given her father while growing up, maybe in the end she had gotten everything she deserved. With that thought more tears began to fall.

Reese had just walked out of the café holding a steaming cup of coffee. It was early and the air was brisk, but nothing smelled better than fresh roasted brew in the morning. He headed for his parked truck, determined to be at the construction site before the men got there this morning. He needed to go over yet another change Marcella Jones had made, but at least thanks to Sebastian Steele, it was a change she would be paying for.

He liked Steele, although he knew Jocelyn hadn't yet gotten used to the guy hanging around. But he felt fairly certain that once she saw he wasn't one of the bad guys she would be okay. His handling of Manuel's situation had proven that he did have a heart.

Reese was about to unlock his truck door and get in when something made him look to the right. He blinked, thinking he was seeing things. Standing a few doors from the café was a woman whose profile so closely resembled Leah's that it was startling. And the more he stared at her, the more he began to realize that it was Leah.

He would know her anywhere, the woman who

MANI
ROMANCE

An Important Message from the Publisher

Dear Reader,

Because you've chosen to read one of our fine novels, I'd like to say "thank you"! And, as a special way to say thank you, I'm offering to send you two more Kimani Romance novels and two surprise gifts – absolutely FREE! These books will keep it real with true-to-life African American characters that turn up the heat and sizzle with passion.

Please enjoy the free books and gifts with our compliments...

Linda Gill

Publisher, Kimani Press

Peel off Seal and Place Inside...

PUBLISHERS
FREE GIFT
SEAL
THANK YOU

THE EDITOR'S "THANK YOU" FREE GIFTS INCLUDE:

▶ Two NEW Kimani Romance™ Novels
▶ Two exciting surprise gifts

YES! I have placed my Editor's "thank you" Free Gifts seal in the space provided at right. Please send me 2 FREE books, and my 2 FREE Mystery Gifts. I understand that I am under no obligation to purchase anything further, as explained on the back of this card.

PLACE
FREE GIFTS
SEAL
HERE

168 XDL EF2F   368 XDL EF2R

FIRST NAME   LAST NAME

ADDRESS

APT.#   CITY

STATE/PROV.   ZIP/POSTAL CODE

Thank You!

The Reader Service — Here's How It Works:

Accepting your 2 free books and gifts places you under no obligation to buy anything. You may keep the books and gifts and return the shipping statement marked "cancel." If you do not cancel, about a month later we'll send you 4 additional books and bill you just $4.69 each in the U.S., or $5.24 each in Canada, plus 25¢ shipping & handling per book and applicable taxes if any.* That's the complete price and --- compared to cover prices of $5.99 each in the U.S. and $6.99 each in Canada --- it's quite a bargain! You may cancel at any time, but if you choose to continue, every month we'll send you 4 more books, which you may either purchase at the discount price or return to us and cancel your subscription.

*Terms and prices subject to change without notice. Sales tax applicable in N.Y. Canadian residents will be charged applicable provincial taxes and GST.

years ago had stolen his heart, just like he would always remember the one night he had made her his in a way no other man had. It had been special for the two of them and—

He immediately forced the thoughts from his mind. That night had been special for him, but evidently not for her, because less than a month later she had left town without looking back. He would never forget the pain he had felt when she'd left. It was pain that still lived in a place deep in his heart, although he wished it would get out of there and leave him alone. He knew that until he was able to let go he would never be worth a damn to any other woman. The thought that Leah had done that to him left a bitter taste in his mouth.

A part of him just wanted to get in the truck and drive away and pretend he hadn't seen her. But for some reason he couldn't do that. The only way he could eradicate Leah from his mind and heart forever finally was to come face to face with her again. He no longer wanted to know why she'd left the way she had, since nothing she said now would matter. He just had to be convinced that he could look her in the face and then turn and walk away.

He took slow steps toward her, and the closer he got the harder his heart began pounding. And when he finally came to stand behind her, he stood without moving since she hadn't noticed his presence. She was too busy studying the items in the store's window. He glanced beyond her to see what had her absolute attention and frowned. It was a baby shop and she was looking at baby clothes. Why would she be doing that?

The next question that skated through his mind was who was pregnant? He didn't like the answer he suddenly came up with. Could the reason Leah wasn't in a hurry to return to California be because she was pregnant?

A blade, sharper than any knife he'd ever handled, sliced through his insides at the thought that she could possibly be carrying a child that wasn't his. He hung his head as pain clouded his thoughts, and he knew he had to get away from there. But something held him transfixed and he knew he had to do this. He had to confront a part of his past that he wished at that moment had never taken place.

Sighing deeply, he took a step closer and noticed Leah was trembling and her shoulders were shaking. Evidently, she was a lot colder than he was.

Deciding not to prolong things, he forced her name from his lips. "Leah?"

Leah's body went stiff, and she hoped more than anything she had imagined the sound of the deep masculine voice. The last thing she needed at that particular moment was to come face to face with the one man who still had a clamp on her heart. The one man she had never stopped loving. The one man she had hurt deeply. And the one man she would never deserve to have again.

"Leah?"

When he said her name a second time, she knew fate was being more than cruel to her today. It was being outright merciless. Pulling in a deep breath, as deep as she could inhale, taking one final swipe at her tears and bracing herself, she slowly turned around while asking God to give her the strength to endure what she knew was going to be one of the hardest moments of her life.

Chapter 8

Nothing could have prepared Reese for the impact of looking into the face of the woman who had shattered his heart into a thousand tiny pieces. Bitterness, anger, hurt and the pain he hadn't been able to let go of suddenly hit him full force, and he almost crushed the hot cup of coffee he held in his hand.

All he could think was that standing before him was the woman who'd once told him she loved him. The woman he had thought he would forever share his life with. The woman destined to be the mother of his children, and the one woman who even now had the love he hadn't been able to share with any other.

The thought that he still loved her, hadn't gotten over her, although he had tried, left a bitter taste in his mouth, left his joints achy with humiliation and made everything within him want to strike out and hurt her as much as she had hurt him. But something was keeping him from doing that. He frowned, seeing the wetness of her eyes and the single tear she'd tried to quickly swipe away. Leah was crying. Why? And why was he even giving a damn?

Then he remembered. She was standing in front of the display window at a baby store. Something about babies had her upset. He quickly jumped back to his earlier suspicion. Was Leah pregnant, and was that the reason she was hanging around?

"Reese, it's good seeing you."

Her words cut into him. The sound of her voice used to send excitement buzzing through every cell in his body. Now it hit a brick wall of resentment. How could she fix her mouth to say it was good seeing him when this was the first time they had come face to face in five years?

He sighed deeply. "I wish I could say the same thing, Leah," he said, his voice low while he fought to keep it steady. "But at the moment, it's not good seeing you again."

Although his words hurt, Leah knew they were what she deserved, and she stood still, feeling the intense anger radiating from him. Jocelyn had warned her, but nothing could have prepared her for this degree of anger. Not from the man who had taught her how to love. The man who had shown her it wasn't always about her but the people she cared about and who cared for her. She'd never got a chance to let him know she'd learned the lessons he had so lovingly taught. The night she was going to commit her heart and soul to him was the same night Neil had assaulted her.

She felt a tear she couldn't fight back slide down her cheek as she met his hostile gaze and said, "I'm sorry you feel that way, Reese."

She watched the frown that formed between his thick eyebrows and saw the narrowing of his eyes. "Why haven't you left yet? There's nothing here for you anymore. You made that decision five years ago, didn't you? That none of us were worthy of your time, consideration…and love."

Her heart clutched as a sharp pain ripped through it. He would think that, wouldn't he? And since he would continue to think that, there was nothing she could say or do to ease the pain or soothe his anger. The best thing to do was to leave.

"I think I'd better go now," she said, not wanting to argue with him. Besides, seeing the fury in his eyes was too much. Reese had always been one of the most easy-going, gentle and loving people she knew. To know he had become a ball of anger because of her was more than she could handle.

"Yeah, go, Leah. Walk away. Leave and don't look back. You're good at that, aren't you?"

She felt more tears well up in her eyes, tears she refused to stand before him and shed. "Yeah, I guess I am. Goodbye, Reese." And as quickly as her legs could carry her, she turned and began walking away. And although it broke her heart, she didn't look back.

"What do you mean we got the wrong tile?"

"Because it's not what we ordered," Harry Henderson answered Jocelyn in disgust. "The box says it's what we ordered but the color is off a shade. See for yourself."

Shaking her head in frustration, Jocelyn put down the saw and went to inspect the box in question. Mason Construction had used Harry exclusively for all their tile work for as long as she could remember. Over the years the older man had brought his son and his grandsons into the business, however, he refused to give up the work and retire.

She often wondered how, at seventy-one, he was able to get on his knees to lay tile. But she had to admit he was still good at what he did and could be depended on more than a lot of the younger workers.

She opened the box and looked in. He was right. These marble tiles had the wrong accent color.

She glanced back up at Harry. "How much of the wrong tile did we get?"

Harry rubbed his bald head, reluctant to tell her. "All thirty boxes, which was supposed to cover over three-hundred square feet."

The entire foyer. Jocelyn breathed in deeply. It was either that or scream. "Let's get the store on the phone."

"I did that already. They apologized for their mistake but said when they called the distributor they were told it's a popular shade that wouldn't be available for six weeks."

"Six weeks! But it was their mistake."

"I told them that. But six weeks was the best they could do."

"That's not good enough," Jocelyn said, seeing red. And it didn't help matters that she hadn't gotten a good night's sleep. "Marcella wants to move into this place in two weeks. Let's skip the distributor and go straight to the manufacturer."

"I did that, too. It's their policy to deal only with the distributor."

"I don't give a hoot about their policy. Give me the number," she said, snatching the cell phone out of her back pocket and punching in the numbers Harry was calling out to her. This was definitely not her morning. They'd had to cancel the committee meeting because three of the members had called at the last minute to say they couldn't make it. And then the traffic light on the corner of Rondell and Marlborough had been out, which had backed traffic up for almost an hour.

Jocelyn sighed when she encountered an auto prompter and had to punch in some more numbers. She glanced up and saw that Harry had had the good sense to get lost for a while after sensing she was getting hotter than fire. Reese would normally handle discrepancies such as this, but the guys told her he'd left to pick up supplies. They'd further told her that he was in a bad mood. She couldn't help but wonder what had Reese's dander up.

A half hour later, her head was spinning and she'd gotten nowhere. The six-week delay still stood.

Jocelyn snapped the phone shut. Didn't businesses believe in providing good customer service anymore?

"So, what's going on?"

She looked up and her eyes collided with those of Bas. For some reason, seeing him made more anger spike through her. He was the reason for her not getting the proper rest last night, and seeing him reminded her of it.

And to make matters even worse, the midday sunlight that was streaming through those windows they'd installed a couple of weeks ago was hitting him at an angle that made an uncomfortable quiver pass through her stomach, not to mention the flush of heat that spread through her body. As usual, he was wearing a pair of jeans and a T-shirt. This time the shirt was rooting for the Pittsburgh Steelers. She frowned, wondering if he had a real allegiance to any team. To any woman.

She shook her head, getting even angrier that she would wonder about such a thing; his love life was no concern of hers.

"Bas to Jocelyn," he said, waving a hand back and forth in front of her face. "Can you read me? You seemed to have zoned out."

Even angrier than before, she folded her arms over her chest. "And where have you been?"

He leaned back against the fireplace mantel and smiled slowly. "I didn't know you wanted me."

What he said and the way he said it sent her pulse into overdrive. It wasn't fair. The man had a sexy physique, he was handsome as all outdoors, and on top of everything else he had a sexy voice that could rival Barry White's any day.

"Did you want me, Jocelyn?"

Sighing deeply, she set her jaw, determined not to say anything. She thought better of it and opened her mouth to tell him a thing or two, but he was quick and placed a finger to her lips. "Remember our truce."

She glared. She didn't care one iota about their so-called truce. Her main concern was tile, namely marble. If Marcella got wind that she would have to wait six weeks for her foyer to be completed, all hell would break loose. A thought suddenly came into Jocelyn's head. Bas was supposed to be the expert troubleshooter, the fixer-upper, the problem solver. So let him deal with it and see if he made more progress than she did.

"We got the wrong tile," she snapped.

He gave her a carefree look. "Then return it."

As if she hadn't been trying to do that for the past half hour. "It'll be another six weeks before the distributor can replace it."

"Tough. We'll go to the manufacturer."

Did he think she hadn't tried that already, too? "I did that," she all but spat out. "And I got nowhere."

"What's the name of the distributor?"

Jocelyn blew out a sharp breath. "Arnett Distributors."

"Arnett Distributors?" He almost laughed. "Then there shouldn't be a problem."

He sounded so convinced she couldn't help but ask, "And why shouldn't there be a problem?"

He smiled again as he met her gaze while pulling out his cell phone and punching in numbers he evidently knew by heart. "Because the Steele Corporation is one of their biggest clients."

Jocelyn nervously chewed the insides of her

cheeks. Could it be possible that Bas had enough clout with Arnett to rectify a major screw-up? She couldn't help remembering the last house they'd done for Marcella Jones and how she claimed the kitchen fixtures hadn't been the ones she'd ordered. She'd pitched such a fit that Jim had taken the six-hour drive to Birmingham and back to pick up the ones Marcella claimed she was supposed to have. Jocelyn didn't relish the thought of having to tell her about the tile.

"Mark Arnett, please."

Bas's words intruded into her thoughts and she wondered how he'd gotten past the auto prompts. She wondered too if he'd gotten any more sleep last night than she had. He didn't seem tired and grouchy this morning. Evidently he hadn't had a restless night remembering how they had indulged in such a mind-blowing kiss. Maybe it had been mind-blowing just to her. Maybe for him it was just so-so.

"Mark? How are you? This is Sebastian Steele. Yes, I'm fine." Then cutting to the chase he said, "Look, I need your help and I want you to put it to the top of your list." He nodded. "Good. There's been a mix-up with a supplier of one of our subsidiary companies and I need it straightened out. I need a particular style of marble tile sent to me right away." There was a pause. "How soon? Overnight if you can."

Another pause. "Here's the style number," he said and began reading the information off the invoice.

"Think you can handle that?" he asked without missing a beat. "Great. Here's the address I want it sent to."

Five minutes later Bas was hanging up the phone, smiling. "Any other fires you want me to put out?"

Not unless he wanted to drop a gallon of water on her head, Jocelyn thought as intense heat ran through every part of her body. While he'd been on the phone with Mark Arnett, trying to save her company from Marcella Jones's wrath, she'd been studying him like a teenager in lust. Every time he moved his body, she got the full effect of seeing him in his tight-fitting jeans and saw how they contoured to his muscular thighs. And if that wasn't bad enough, that Pittsburgh Steelers T-shirt was clearly emphasizing muscular arms, a firm flat chest and nice wide shoulders. Display Bas on a poster and she would buy whatever he was advertising.

"Jocelyn?"

Snatched out of her reverie, she lifted her chin and straightened her shoulders. "No, there aren't any more fires you need to put out. Thanks."

"Don't mention it." He glanced around. "Where's Reese?"

"Doing a pickup."

He blew out a breath and frowned. "When do you expect him back?"

She lifted a brow. "Not sure. Is anything wrong?"

"No, just have him call the office when he returns."

For some reason Jocelyn felt he wasn't telling her everything. Why did he want to talk to Reese? He was just the foreman. She was the one in charge of things. Maybe she needed to remind him of that.

"Look," she said, leaning closer and looking intently at him.

"Yes?" he said, and she felt the force of his own gaze back.

"You do remember who's in charge, don't you?"

He smiled. "Yeah, I think so, but do you want to remind me again?"

She frowned, and suddenly wanted to find the hammer and clobber him. "I'm trying to be nice."

"You shouldn't have to try so hard. It should come naturally," he said and reached out and tweaked her nose. "I'll see you later."

She was ready to throw out an angry retort when she saw that Harry had reappeared and the two of them were talking with obvious familiarity. Evidently they remembered each other from that summer Bas had worked with her father. Jocelyn decided what she had to say to Bas could wait. There was no need to put him in his place in front of Harry. She would have enough time to read him later.

She was pulled away from those thoughts when her cell phone rang. "Yes?"

"Is Reese there?"

She recognized Leah's voice immediately. "No. Why?"

"Because I saw him this morning."

She could tell from the tone of her sister's voice that there was more. "And?"

"And we had words."

Jocelyn felt her throat tighten. "Not so nice ones, I gather."

"You gathered right."

Jocelyn nodded. No wonder Reese was in a bad mood. Now she understood why the men thought he was angry about something. "Are you okay?" she asked, concerned.

"Yes, but barely. And you were right. He hates me."

"I never said he hated you. I said he was still hurting."

"Same difference, since I'm the one who hurt him."

There was a pause because Jocelyn didn't know what to say. No, that wasn't true. She did know what to say, but she also knew Leah wouldn't want to hear it. She trailed a finger along the fine craftsmanship of the wooden banister Reese had completed last week. "I still think you should tell him the truth."

"I can't."

She decided not to press when she heard the trembling in Leah's voice. She didn't have to see her sister's face to know she'd been crying and probably still was. "Hey, how about the two of us doing something tonight?"

"Like what?"

"Going to a movie."

"A movie?"

"Yes, a movie. When was the last time we went to a movie together?" She could just imagine Leah bunching up her forehead trying to remember.

"Um, I think it was when Aunt Susan took us to see *Titanic*."

"Hey, you're right," Jocelyn said smiling as she remembered. "She really liked that picture, didn't she?"

"Yes, she did. We sat through it twice. After that I didn't care if I ever saw the ocean again."

"I felt the same way." Jocelyn laughed.

"You know," Leah then said in a quiet voice, "I wish she had been around five years ago. I would have gone to Florida instead of California. For all her proper ways, Aunt Susan was pretty special, wasn't she?"

Jocelyn nodded. "Yes, she was." After a brief pause she said, "So how about it? Do you want to do a movie?"

She heard Leah chuckle and liked the sound. "Will going to a movie help you sleep better tonight?" Leah asked with a hint of teasing in her voice.

Jocelyn glanced across the room to Bas. He was still talking to Harry. And as if he felt her eyes on him, he tilted his head and looked at her. The deep intensity of his dark gaze was pinning her to the spot, heating her even more.

It was hard for Jocelyn to keep her voice steady when she replied, "No guarantees there, but it's worth a try."

Bas threw the file aside and glanced at his watch. It was almost four in the afternoon. He had a ton of files he still needed to review so there was no reason for Jocelyn Mason to be on his mind.

But she was.

Muttering a curse he leaned back in the chair and picked up a file he had placed to the side. He had done the accounting three times and still the figures weren't right, but before he jumped to any conclusions, he would do as Jim had instructed him in another letter that Kilgore had dropped off a few days ago. All the note had said was: Talk to Reese first about any discrepancies you may find in the bookkeeping records.

Then, just that quickly, he dismissed the note from his mind as his thoughts wandered to Jocelyn again. He had known she was troubled by something the moment he'd seen her. It was there in her face. She'd had that worried look. And ridiculous as it seemed, something deep within him had wanted to get rid of whatever was causing her stress.

Luckily all it had taken was a phone call and the use of his connections to make things right and to remove her troubled frown. But as usual, they had almost gotten into another argument, something he hadn't been up to. After talking with Harry he had quickly left, eager to be gone from Jocelyn's presence before she found another bone to pick. After a sleepless night and dealing with Sadie that morning, he hadn't been in the best of moods, either. The last thing they needed was to be at each other's throats…or lips.

Damn, but he couldn't get their kiss out of his mind! He shook his head remembering. Whoever said 'out of sight, out of mind' didn't know what the hell they were talking about, he thought, reaching for an apple from the basket of fresh fruit Sadie Robinson had dropped off a few moments ago. The woman had stayed only long enough to lecture him on how much better fruit was than some of the other snacks she'd noticed him gobbling up. He hadn't found her spiel amusing but Noreen, Mason Construction's secretary, had.

Noreen Telfair.

The woman's name suddenly made him recall the accounting issue and why he needed to talk to Reese. The one thing he'd noticed about the attractive woman was that she appeared to be a good worker who didn't have much to say. He knew that she was in her late forties, a divorcée with a teenage daughter, and that she had moved to town three or four years ago from Atlanta. He'd discovered that bit of info from reading her employee records, which was something he had taken the time to do on everyone who worked at Mason's.

"The guys said you were looking for me."

Bas glanced up when Reese walked into what used to be Jim's office. Bas took one look at Reese, saw his tense expression and immediately knew something was bothering him. "Hey, man, you okay?"

"Yeah, I'm fine," he said, closing the door behind him and crossing the room to sit in a leather chair. "Today's been a rough one."

Bas chuckled. "Tell me about it." He was pretty good at reading people, and although Reese had said things were fine, Bas knew that something wasn't. But he was a person who made it a point not to get involved in anyone else's business unless he was asked.

He leaned forward, remembering why he needed to see Reese. "I was going through the accounting records and found several discrepancies. Kilgore delivered a letter to me a couple of days ago that Jim left. In it were instructions that I talk to you first if I found problems with the books."

Reese sat up straighter in his chair as a confused expression covered his face. "Jim said that?"

"Yes."

"I wonder why. As far as I know I'm not privy to any information regarding Mason Construction's accounting records. What's the discrepancy?"

"Several deposits of large amounts were placed in an account for Noreen. The last one was a couple of months before Jim died. I verified the signature and he signed off on all of them, but he doesn't note in the records what they were for."

"Oh," Reese said and then sat back and smoothed his hands along the arms of the chair. "I don't know exactly what they were for, but I have an idea."

"All right," Bas said, sensing Reese's hesitancy in discussing the matter. "Was it a loan? Blackmail? Help me to understand, Reese. We're talking about a total of over a hundred thousand dollars here."

Reese shifted nervously in his chair and met the intensity in Bas's gaze. "No one was supposed to know and I only found out by accident."

Bas lifted a brow. "You found out what by accident?"

Reese shifted in his chair again and lowered his eyes when he spoke. "That Jim and Noreen were lovers."

Bas didn't so much as blink since that had been

one of his suspicions. "Why did they keep it a secret? Jim was a widower and Noreen is divorced."

Reese shrugged and met Bas's eyes. "Yes, but there's the issue of the difference in their ages. We're talking about fifteen years. And besides that, this is a small town that sometimes feeds on gossip, and Noreen has a teenage daughter they wanted to protect. They were very discreet and most of the time they planned out-of-town trips. They had been together a couple of years before I found out. I happened to be visiting a cousin in Atlanta when I ran into the two of them in a hotel there. Needless to say, it was a very uncomfortable moment because it was the last thing I'd suspected."

Bas nodded. "Did Jocelyn know?"

"I doubt it. At least Jim and Noreen assumed she didn't know. I really don't think she would have had a problem with it had she known. But like I said, Jim was uncomfortable about the difference in their ages. Noreen didn't have a problem with it."

"And they were lovers until he died?"

"Yes, and I really thought things would come out then, but Jim made Noreen promise not to say or do anything to give them away. That part was pretty hard on her."

"I'm sure it was."

"And he didn't want to leave her a big chunk in his will like he did for me, to give everyone a reason to speculate why. That's why he set up a special account for her in this bank in Memphis. She didn't know he was doing it until right before he died."

"I see."

"That's probably why he wanted you to come in and check out things before Jocelyn got a mind to call in an independent accountant to audit the records."

Bas leaned back in his chair. "Thanks for sharing that with me. That clears up a lot."

"Well, Noreen and Jim cared a lot for each other and although their affair wasn't made public, they made each other happy, and to me that's all that mattered. For some people happiness is a rare commodity these days."

Bas said nothing for a moment after hearing the rancor in Reese's voice. He remembered having to deal with his brother's Morgan's bitterness a few months ago when a woman he was interested in refused even to discuss the possibility of them pursuing a relationship.

Bas quickly made a decision about something. He might as well call it a day since he wasn't thinking about work much anyway. "So, what are your plans for the rest of the day, Reese?"

Reese stood. "I'm going over to the gym to work out awhile. I feel like hitting something and I prefer it to be a punching bag than a human being."

Bas nodded. He knew the feeling. He remembered passing the gym when he arrived in town. It seemed like a pretty new facility. He couldn't remember the last time he gave his body a good workout. "Mind if I join you?"

Reese smiled. "No, not at all."

"Good. I'll run by Sadie's and get my gear and then meet you there in about thirty minutes." Bas locked the files in the drawer for the night.

Beating up on a punching bag wasn't such a bad idea.

Chapter 9

This was the part of construction she loved the best. The finish. Or in this case, the part that was pretty close to being finished, because with Marcella Jones you never knew for sure. But since Bas had explained their pay-if-you-make-any-changes policy, she had kept the changes to a minimum. In fact she had made barely any at all.

Jocelyn glanced around with her hand on her hips. This was indeed a beautiful home and she could imagine how grand it would look furnished. Marcella wasn't known to skimp when it came to getting what she wanted so there was no doubt in Jocelyn's mind that this house would be the talk of the town for a while…at least until Marcella saw another design for a home that suited her fancy in one of those magazines of hers. Then there would be house number four.

"It looks nice, doesn't it?"

Jocelyn turned and smiled at Reese. "Yes, it does, and from the look of things, we'll finish on time. That marble tile came this morning and Harry and his crew have already put it down. They'll be back tomorrow to grout it."

She then studied Reese with concern in her eyes. She hadn't seen him yesterday and wondered if he was okay. "And how are you, Reese? Leah told me you saw each other yesterday."

Jocelyn watched as bitterness lined his lips. "Yes, we did. I should have been prepared but I wasn't," he said quietly.

"And I don't think she was prepared, either."

Reese's dark eyes flashed. "Then that's tough for her, isn't it?" He inhaled deeply and said, "Look, Jocelyn, I'd rather not discuss Leah, but there is something I need to know. If you can't tell me, then I'll understand."

"What?"

Reese hung his head and studied the gleaming wood floor for a second then met Jocelyn's gaze again. "Is Leah pregnant? Is that the reason she's not in a hurry to leave here?"

Of all the questions she had expected him to ask that sure wasn't one. "What gave you an idea like that? She definitely doesn't look pregnant."

"No, but yesterday morning I walked up on her staring into the display window of that baby store in town…and she was crying."

"Oh." Jocelyn pressed a hand to her chest as if she could feel her sister's pain. Poor Leah. She hadn't been crying for what she had, but for what she thought she could never have—Reese's child.

"Well, is she pregnant?"

She heard the anger in his voice and the pain. The thought that Leah might be pregnant with another man's child had to be hurting him deeply. At least that was one pain Jocelyn could take away. "No, she's not pregnant."

"How do you know for sure? She might be and just hasn't told you."

"Because I know," she snapped, feeling the need to come to Leah's defense, considering everything. "She can't be pregnant."

Reese frowned deeply. "You don't know that."

"I do know that," she said, rounding on him angrily. "She hasn't been involved with anyone since you and—" Jocelyn stopped abruptly, fearing she might have said too much.

"What the hell do you mean she hasn't been involved with anyone since me? Do you actually believe that lie?" he asked incredulously. "I never thought you of all people would be that gullible."

Jocelyn's eyes flashed fire. "Yes, I believe it because…"

He lifted a brow. "Because what?"

Disgusted with herself and the entire situation and knowing if Neil Grunthall wasn't dead already he would have been by the end of the day, she released a frustrated sigh. "Look, Reese, forget I said anything."

"What are you not telling me, Jocelyn?" he asked, grabbing her arm.

She snatched it back, although it cost her to do so. She would love for him to know what she wasn't telling him. "Look, let it be, okay? All you need to know is that Leah isn't pregnant." She turned to leave but Reese called out to her and she turned back around. "What?"

"Just in case I don't see you in the morning, I'm cutting out a little early tomorrow. Two of Bas's brothers are coming in and I plan to take them up to Cedar Springs for the weekend to do a little fishing."

"Fine," she said, shoving both hands into the pockets of her jeans. "Enjoy yourselves."

Then she turned back around and continued walking.

"Thanks for a great weekend, Reese," Bas said on Sunday afternoon as he got out of Reese's truck and gathered his belongings. "There were good lodgings, good company, good fishing and damn good beer. What more can a man ask for?"

"Nothing's wrong with a good woman every now and then," Reese answered, grinning.

"Hell, but not on a fishing trip. They get too squeamish and want you to have pity and throw your catch back. Women and fishing don't mix."

Reese gave a smooth laugh. "You must have never gone fishing with the right woman. Leah could handle just—" He stopped suddenly, then said. "Oh, hell, dammit to three degrees. I promised myself that I wouldn't mention her name, much less think about her this weekend. She's not worth the effort."

Bas shook his head. "Evidently she is. What has it been? Five years? And you're still carrying a torch? That was some kind of love."

Reese's hand tightened on the steering wheel. It would be useless to deny he was still carrying a torch. "Yeah, and she didn't deserve any of it."

"Seems you haven't convinced your heart of that yet. See you around, buddy."

Moments later Bas entered the cabin he had purchased with his brothers' blessings as investment property for the Steele Corporation. Reese, Morgan and Donovan had helped him to move in Friday afternoon then they had left to go fishing Saturday morning.

He couldn't help but ponder the fact that Reese was still in love with a woman who had torn out his heart and stomped on it. Bas was damn grateful he had never been in love. Even when he was engaged to Cassandra, he'd liked her, been fond of her, but not once did he think he loved her. Their marriage would have been a sort of business arrangement. With thirty staring her in the face, she wanted a husband who could keep her in the lifestyle she was accustomed to, and he'd wanted a proper lady who was refined as well as beautiful. What he hadn't been looking for but what he'd found in Cassandra had also been snobbery to a degree he just couldn't tolerate.

A half hour later, after taking a very relaxing shower, Bas walked out of the bathroom. Wrapped in a towel, not yet ready to put on any clothes, he crossed the room to look out the window, liking the view. Mountains in the distance and a small stream out back provided a picturesque scene. This could be a place he, his brothers or cousins could use when they just wanted to get away. Privacy was golden sometimes, and everybody needed it on occasion.

When he'd told Ms. Sadie that he had purchased the cabin and would be moving, she had smiled and made him promise to eat properly. But he had a feeling she would continue to show up at the office at lunch time with a fruit basket for him. In a way he looked forward to her visits, even realizing he actually enjoyed eating fruit.

After a few moments, Bas suddenly felt antsy and considered driving to the office to work on more files, but he quickly decided against it. This had been a relaxing weekend, and he didn't want to spoil it. He couldn't help the smile that touched his lips at that moment. He had been glad to see Morgan and Donovan, although he would never admit it to them. And Reese had been the perfect host. The four of them had fished to their hearts' content, drunk as much beer as their bellies could hold and talked about anything and everything…except women. They hadn't had much time to think of women, either.

But now, back in the privacy of his little place, Bas's mind was once again filled with thoughts of Jocelyn. He couldn't help wondering what she was doing. Had she thought of him any this weekend? Was the kiss they'd shared a few nights ago still seared on her brain the same way it was on his?

His lips quirked. There was only one way to find out. He wanted to see her. He needed to see her. Damn, he needed to kiss her again. He grinned. This was the first time he'd ever gotten addicted to a woman's taste and he wasn't sure what he was going to do about it other than feed his habit.

* * *

"So you're Sebastian Steele."

Bas nodded. If the woman who'd opened the door to him was Leah Mason, then he could understand why after five years Reese hadn't been able to eradicate her from his heart. She was a woman a man wouldn't be able to forget easily. But then so was her sister.

"Yes, I'm Sebastian and you're Leah, right?"

"Yes, I'm Leah. I'm glad I finally got to meet you. I've heard a lot about you."

Bas refused to throw out the cliché "all good I hope," since he knew if it came from Jocelyn that would not have been the case. "And I'm glad I finally got to meet you," he said slipping his hands into his pockets. "I was wondering if Jocelyn is home."

Leah smiled. "Yes, she's home but not here. She's at her place right outside of town. Do you know where that is?"

"Yes, I think I do." In all honesty, the day she had taken him there he had been too busy trying to survive the truck ride to care about the direction in which she'd been driving.

"It's real easy to find," she said, giving him instructions.

"Thanks."

"You're welcome. I'd like to invite you over for dinner one night when you're free. Dad thought a lot of you and I'd like to get to know you better."

"Thanks and the same here. Good night."

"Good night."

When she closed the door, Bas turned and quickly walked back to his car. More than anything he wanted to see Jocelyn.

Leah smiled, wondering if she should give Jocelyn a call to prepare her for Sebastian Steele's visit, then decided not to. Whether her sister admitted it or not she knew something was going on between those two. She smiled and went to the sofa to settle back down with her book.

She'd never known Jocelyn to have a boyfriend. Oh, she had gone out on dates but had never gotten serious about anyone. Now it looked like that history was about to change.

Jocelyn tapped a finger to her lips as she glanced around the room. She had gone shopping yesterday and purchased this beautiful hand-carved vase, and she wasn't quite certain of the best spot for it.

The coffee table or the bookcase?

She was leaning toward the coffee table when her doorbell sounded. She automatically assumed it was Rita, Reese's brother's wife from across the lake.

Instead of asking who it was, she snatched open the door, only to find Sebastian Steele. His tall, broad-shouldered frame lounged against her porch rail, a dark silhouette, barely distinguishable in the faint light spilling out from her foyer.

Caught completely by surprise, she needed a moment before she could say anything. When she found her voice she said, "I usually don't open the door before finding out who it is first. I assumed you were my neighbor."

His lips twitched briefly. "I thought we had a serious discussion about the dangers of assuming anything."

She tipped her head and stared at him. Emotions she didn't need or want began clogging her throat. "What are you doing here, Bas?" she asked tightly. She hadn't seen him in three days and she wished to God she hadn't been counting. But she had.

Bas pushed away from the rail and took a couple of steps forward. He figured if he were to tell her the real reason for his visit—that he wanted to devour her mouth—the door would get slammed in his face, so instead he said, "It's early. I didn't want to go to the office, and I wasn't ready to go to bed yet. We had a great weekend down at Cedar Springs and I could only think of one way to end it."

"And what way is that?" Jocelyn's fingers tightened around the doorknob. Her mind was suddenly filled with forbidden yet romantic thoughts. Bas's gaze was locked on hers and she was beginning to feel this luscious, hot sensation flow all through her.

She even felt the floor beneath her feet give way a little. A small smile tugged at the corner of his mouth, and in response she felt something tug deep in the pit of her stomach. Her world began to rock and she waited with bated breath for his reply.

"A rematch. I want to play another game of pinball with you."

Chapter 10

Jocelyn drew a breath, leaned in the doorway and stared at Bas. She guessed she should have been grateful that a game of pinball was all he had in mind but still… It wasn't helping matters that since meeting him and sharing two kisses, her body had become somewhat treacherous whenever he was around.

Her system automatically went on overload and it took everything she could muster to retain the common sense she was born with and had kept intact over the years. But another part of her being reminded her that she'd been celibate for a very long time…ever since senior year in college over six years ago. Why let the explosive spontaneous combustion she felt with Bas go to waste?

Because you're too sensible and dignified to play the games men want to play, she assured herself immediately. Although she was single, mature and unattached, with basic human urges like the next person, that didn't mean she was into casual sex. When the time came for a man to touch her again, by golly it would mean something and not be an appeasement of curiosity like the last time, which had left her totally disappointed.

"So you want to play pinball?" she finally asked, cocking her brow. "Didn't you learn anything from our last game?"

He flashed a quick grin. "Oh yeah, I learned a lot. I know not to let my guard down again."

"Is that what happened?"

"Yes. I concentrated more on you than the game."

She hadn't expected him to admit that. "So what's your game plan this time?"

"Do you really expect me to tell you?"

She chuckled. "No, but I thought it wouldn't hurt to ask." She stepped aside. "Come on in and let the game begin."

An hour or so later Jocelyn glanced over at Bas and narrowed her eyes. He was leading by over one hundred thousand points and she was the one who was finding it hard to concentrate on the game. Frustration began to surface. It wasn't that she didn't like losing; she just didn't like the reason she was losing—her inability to focus.

"Winning this rematch means a lot to you, doesn't it?" she finally asked when he scored once again.

He grinned over at her. "Worried about losing?"

"No. But it does seem like you're deliberately dragging this game out."

"While staying ahead in points."

"For the moment, yes."

"Um, I'm just consolidating my shots and economizing my ball time," he said. "A strategy that works best for me."

"You're working too hard as usual," she said coming to stand close to him, but not close enough to mess with his concentration. "All I do is focus on the shots I can hit consistently and patiently repeat them. In a game of pinball you can never lose control."

"Or concentration, so please step back, Jocelyn. Your perfume is getting to me."

"Is it?"

"Yes."

"In what way?"

His eyes flashed to hers. "I don't think you really want to know."

Jocelyn raised an arched brow. Did she or didn't she? She was pulled out of her thoughts by his muttered curse. He hadn't used his flippers fast enough and it was now her turn.

"Move over Steele. Time for me to recoup."

Deciding not to crowd her, Bas took the chair a few feet away and watched her in action. He liked seeing the way her eyes sparkled with the feel of victory and the way she licked her lips each time she deployed a ball. Then there was that simple turn of her head, the smile that tilted her lips whenever she hit a shot that made the machine flash.

And last but definitely not least was the way she leaned her body just so to the machine, breasts perked, hips aligned at an angle that had heat drumming through him. Even with her trying to best him at this game, he detected a gracefulness in the ease in which she was attempting to do so. The woman had style, something he noted even when she was holding a hammer, saw or a drill.

She had taste. And she tasted good.

He rubbed a hand over his face wishing he hadn't thought about her taste.

When the machine flashed that the game was over, he barely heard her unladylike curse, which let him know he had won this go-round.

"Want to do another game?"

He smiled. "No, we agreed on five and I won four of the five, which means I'm on top of you this time."

Although Jocelyn knew what he meant by those

words, her mind suddenly conjured up something else and heat clawed viciously at the lower part of her stomach. She could just imagine him naked and on top of her beneath silken sheets. "Okay, so now I want a rematch," she said, needing to get her mind back on track and wondering how she had allowed it to veer into such an outlandish fantasy in the first place.

"I'll think about it."

Her eyes flamed. "What do you mean you'll think about it?"

He stood and slowly walked in front of her. "Just what I said." He smiled. "Now who's the sore loser?"

"I'm not a sore loser," she denied.

"Then why are you mad?"

"I'm not mad."

"If not, you're awfully close," he said in a husky tone.

He reached out and took her hand in his, letting his fingers run across her wrist to feel her pulse. "Those are anger beats."

"They're not," she said, refusing to let the feel of his finger on her wrist unnerve her, stoke a desire she didn't want to acknowledge.

"And why are your eyes getting so dark if you aren't mad?" he asked in an even deeper tone of voice.

"They aren't getting dark."

"Yes, they are and getting even darker as we speak." The hand that wasn't stroking her wrist reached up and framed her face. "And why are your lips trembling if you aren't mad?"

She frowned. "You're seeing things."

He leaned in a little closer and let a single fingertip trace a path down to the base of her throat. "No, Jocelyn. I'm feeling things and I think it's time you felt them, too."

Suddenly, the air around them seemed to thicken as he leaned closer and lowered his mouth to hers. The moment their lips touched, lust of an intensity Jocelyn had never known flamed to life, and everything inside her, every cell, every pore, quivered with totally unique and unexpected pleasure.

When his tongue plundered her mouth, she felt her knees slipping and her nipples tingling against her blouse. Just as before, his tongue was in control, taking, giving and sharing. It was the most conducive pleasure mechanism she had ever felt, and with each and every stroke it was hitting its mark. She was beginning to feel drunk, intoxicated, just plain loose. He smelled good. The scent of him was going straight to her head and the taste of him was getting absorbed in areas she'd rather not think about. This kiss was different from the others, though. It was slow, deep, provoking. And overwhelming. Each time he mated his tongue with hers, captured it, sucked on it, she heard herself moan.

Reluctantly Bas broke the kiss, inhaled deeply

before drawing her closer to him. He needed that. He needed her. He wanted to touch her a little while longer, let his hands skim slowly across her back. Apparently she felt at ease in letting him do so because she stood still, wrapped in his arms, in his heat.

Moments later, she pulled back, angled her head and gazed up at him and smiled slowly. Her eyes were still dark, her lips moist from his kiss. "If you're trying to make me forget that I want a rematch, forget it."

He released a soft chuckle and leaned down to let his lips brush against hers again, needing the taste, the feel, the touch. "Then I'm going to have to perfect my technique."

She doubted he could perfect it any more, but she wouldn't tell him that. "You can try."

"And I will." Bas smiled. He liked the art of seduction as much as the next guy, although he hadn't had to contemplate a plan in quite a while. They weren't talking about pinball anymore but something else, and they both knew it.

"Don't consider it, Bas," she warned, as if reading his thoughts. "We'll drive each other crazy. I like enjoying life, having fun. You're determined to work yourself to death."

He shook his head. "Hey, I've loosened up some."

She chuckled. "So I see, but you need to do it even more. Just think of all the fun you're missing."

He gazed at her for a moment. He had enjoyed the workout at the gym with Reese the other day. He had definitely relieved a lot of stress. And going fishing this past weekend had been great, and playing pinball tonight had been just what he'd needed. But nothing could compare to kissing her. That had been like putting the icing on the cake. An idea suddenly popped into his mind.

"You want to show me how to have fun?"

He could tell his question surprised her, and he watched as she lifted a brow. "Not sure that I can."

He leaned closer to her and let his lips brush against her moist ones again. "Don't you want to try?" he asked, nibbling on her neck. "Unless you don't think you can handle me." He knew that would be a challenge she couldn't let slide.

"Oh, I can handle you, Sebastian Steele."

"Prove it," he whispered in her ear. "Teach me how to have fun, Jocelyn."

A deep, gentle trembling in the pit of her stomach answered before her lips could. "Be careful what you ask for Bas…but since you *did* ask, I'm going to take you on." She took a step back. "The first thing you have to do is stop work every day at five o' clock."

He looked at her as though she had lost her mind. "Five o'clock?"

"Yes."

He thought again about the time he'd spent at the gym. He could do that a couple of days a week in the afternoons. No big deal. "All right."

A frown drew Jocelyn's brows together. He was being too agreeable and she was wondering what was going through his mind. "And you can't arrive at the office before nine in the morning," she decided to add just to cover all her bases.

She saw the defiance that sparked his eyes and grinned in spite of herself. He had only agreed to quit work at five because he'd intended to arrive at some ungodly hour every morning. She could tell he didn't like that she was one step ahead of him.

"And next weekend, there's a jazz festival in Memphis. You want to go have fun?" she asked, deciding to make him see that she meant business.

He shrugged. "Sure." And then he asked, "When do I get to come up with some of our fun activities?" A gleam shone in the depths of his eyes. "I think we should take turns coming up with stuff."

She nodded, thinking that would be only fair, but of course she would monitor the stuff he came up with. She knew men had a tendency to take advantage of what they perceived as a golden opportunity. "I don't have a problem with that. Do you have something in mind?"

He smiled as he grabbed his jacket off the back of the chair and slipped his arms in the sleeves. His gaze held hers when he said, "Yes, I have a few ideas."

She lifted a brow. "Should I be worried?"

He chuckled. "Of course not. You're going to have to trust me like I'm going to trust you." He leaned over and kissed her again, slow, thorough, and as if he desperately needed the memory.

"Come walk me to the door," he whispered and she shivered when his tongue snaked out and trailed a wet path from her lips to an area beneath her ear.

Jocelyn could barely walk up the steps on unsteady legs and knew that after Bas left it would take the rest of the night to recover from his visit.

"So, I take it Sebastian Steele found you last night."

Jocelyn lifted her eyebrows and gazed across the breakfast table at her sister. Jocelyn had arrived at her father's home a little more than thirty minutes ago to find Leah preparing breakfast. "What made you think he was looking for me?"

Leah smiled. "Because he came here first and then I directed him to your place. He's a cutie."

"Yes, he is," Jocelyn muttered and went back to eating her meal.

Amused, Leah watched her sister. She knew Jocelyn wouldn't volunteer any information so she decided to go ahead and pick it out of her. "So, are the two of you an item?"

The thought of that made Jocelyn choke on her toast and she quickly grabbed her glass of juice and took a gulp. "Whatever gave you that idea?"

Leah shrugged. "The obvious. He's good-looking and so are you. He's unattached and so are you. He's—"

"What makes you think he's unattached?" Jocelyn asked, setting down her juice glass.

Leah waved her left hand. "No ring. That's a sure sign."

"But not a concrete one."

Leah's eyes lifted. "You think he's married?"

"No, I don't think he's married."

"Then you think he has a girlfriend?"

"There's that possibility."

"Have you asked him about it?"

"No."

"Then I most certainly will."

"Why would you want to know?"

Leah rolled her eyes. "I don't want to know for myself. I want to know for you."

Jocelyn pushed her plate aside and leaned forward. "And why would you want to know for me?"

"Because you're interested in him. I can tell."

Jocelyn narrowed her eyes. "I hate to tell you that you're wrong, but you are. I admit Bas is handsome, but he's not my type."

"If you say so."

"I do, so let's change the subject."

"All right."

Jocelyn didn't miss how her sister's lips curved in a smile. "So, did you decide whether you want to go to the jazz festival in Memphis this coming weekend? I invited Bas along."

"You want me to make it a threesome?"

Jocelyn shook her head. "I told him it's nothing like that. In fact I'm supposed to show him how to have fun."

"Sounds interesting."

"It is, so do you want to go?"

"No, I'll pass. Besides, I need to start packing."

Surprise showed on Jocelyn's face. "You're leaving?"

"Eventually, Jocelyn. I need to start looking for another place to stay in California. I already told you that the lady whom I used to be a companion to died a couple of months ago. Her sons have been more than kind by letting me remain in the house for a while, but I can't take advantage of their generosity forever."

"You can come back and live here, you know," Jocelyn said, and gestured to encompass the house they were in. "If you don't, I'll eventually have to rent it out or sell it. I don't relish the thought of people I don't know living here."

Leah sighed deeply. "I wish I could move back home, but I can't."

Jocelyn didn't need to ask her why. "Leah, if you were to tell him what—"

"No. And I don't want to talk about it, Jocelyn," Leah said in a clear and distinct voice.

Jocelyn drew in a deep breath. She wanted so much for Leah, more than her sister was willing to accept as a way of life. If only she would tell Reese the truth.

"To hang around here any longer will be a mistake, Jocelyn."

"So you're planning to leave?"

"Yes, in a few weeks. I'm going to start checking out airline tickets later today."

"I really do wish you'd consider staying."

"And I really wish that you'll understand that I can't." That said, Leah rose gracefully, proving all of their Aunt Susan's teachings were still intact, and left the room.

"You're going to Memphis this weekend with Jocelyn?" Reese asked, tipping his head to one side to stare at Bas.

Bas pushed aside the stack of files. It was four-thirty and if he intended to keep his word to Jocelyn, he had thirty minutes left before calling it a day. "Yes. And if it wasn't for that, I'd love going to the horse races this weekend with you and your brother."

Reese's lips twitched in amusement. "I can't wait until Duran Law hears about you and Jocelyn's weekend plans. He's been trying to get her to go to that jazz festival with him in Memphis for years and she's always turned him down. Now, just like that," he said, snapping his fingers for effect, "you breeze into town and talk her into going." Reese chuckled. "Yeah, old Duran is going to be pretty pissed."

Bas leaned back in his chair. "Actually the trip was her idea. She thinks I need to incorporate more fun into my life." Then, without missing a beat he asked, "And who's this Duran Law anyway? An old boyfriend?"

Reese snorted. "He wished. Duran's been a pain in Jocelyn's ass since high school. I guess he figures sooner or later he'll wear down her defenses, and he's too into himself to see that something like that won't happen."

Bas frowned, not liking the man already. "How are things going over at the Jones place?"

"Great. We hope to have our walk-through next week. But keep your fingers crossed. We're yet to have one on time for Marcella. She likes finding things for us to correct or change at the eleventh hour."

"Yeah, we'll all keep our fingers crossed." Bas then glanced at his watch.

"Ready to head over to the gym?" Reese asked.

"In a few seconds. I need to touch base with my brother about something."

"Okay, I'll meet you over there."

"Will do."

Bas pulled out his cell phone, pressed one number and within seconds he heard his brother Chance's deep voice. "Bas? What's going on?"

Before Bas could answer, Chance said, "Hey, hold on and let me take this other call." And then he clicked off.

Bas knew what a busy schedule his brother had as CEO of the corporation, but he smiled, thinking that time restraints hadn't gotten in the way of him pursuing Kylie once he'd become interested. To kill time while waiting for Chance, Bas glanced around Jim's office. There were numerous trophies proclaiming him to be Builder of the Year and several plaques awarded for his community service and involvement in such worthwhile organizations such as the Boy Scouts, Big Dads of America, the Newton Grove Mission and others. Apparently Jim hadn't had any qualms about occasionally putting his work aside to become involved in things he felt were important to him, activities that gave him enjoyment and the chance to do something other than work. *Fun* things.

"Sorry about that, Bas. That was a call I was waiting on from the Evans Group."

Bas lifted a brow. The Evans Group was currently in a bitter labor dispute with the Teamsters Union regarding a number of their employees who had been laid off. "Something going on I need to know about?"

"No, not now, but I'll keep you posted."

"Yeah, you do that. I know you're busy so I won't hold you. I just want to know if things are still on for Donovan's birthday party."

"Yes, Vanessa and Kylie are taking care of all the arrangements, but as far as I know they're on track. I talked to Taylor and Cheyenne and they're both flying in. Should be nice. You are coming home for it, aren't you?"

"Yes, and I might be bringing somebody with me."

"Oh, who?"

"Jocelyn Mason. I haven't asked her yet, but it'll be my turn to come up with some fun activity for us to do."

"Fun activity? Bas, what are you talking about?"

Bas chuckled, knowing his brother was confused. "I'll explain things the next time we talk. Just let Kylie and Vanessa know that I might be bringing a guest. I'll know for certain after this weekend."

"Okay, I'll pass on the word. Take care, Bas."

"You do the same."

After putting his cell phone away, Bas glanced at his watch. It was five o'clock on the dot. He bade Noreen a good afternoon when he passed her office, and walked out of the building while it was still daylight. Amazing.

The September evening was rather chilly and he

pulled his leather jacket tighter around his body. He hadn't seen Jocelyn that day and had avoided dropping by the job site. It would be hard seeing her and not wanting a repeat performance of the kiss they'd shared last night. The art of kissing had always interested him, and depending on his partner, he usually varied his technique. Cassandra had gotten put off by the use of too much tongue. She liked her kisses the same way she wanted everything else they did that was connected to sex—in moderation. According to her, a true lady didn't get carried away with passion, especially with a kiss. It was just unthinkable.

He chuckled, glad not *all* true ladies thought that way. And Jocelyn was a true lady, hard hat, jeans, work boots and all. There was that gracefulness about her even when she was wielding a hammer. She was soft but not mushy. Regal but not overly so and she definitely wasn't a snob. But what he enjoyed most was how much she liked kissing—just as much as he did. And because she did, he'd never enjoyed kissing any woman as much as he enjoyed kissing her. One aspect of that realization disturbed him, while another kept constant heat drumming through his body.

Smiling, he couldn't help but look forward to the coming weekend.

Chapter 11

"If I didn't know better I'd think you were trying to avoid me this week."

A slow smile curved Jocelyn's lips as she snapped her seat belt in place. She glanced over at Bas and squinted her eyes against the glare of the sun peeking over the mountains. "Now why would you think that?"

Bas stared out of the windshield of his car for a second before tilting his head to meet her gaze. "Because this is the first time I've seen you since Sunday night."

"But we talked on the phone Wednesday," she reminded him.

"Yes, all of five minutes," he murmured, backing the car out of her driveway. "And that was to tell me this would be an overnight trip and you had made reservations for us at a hotel. With *separate* sleeping arrangements."

Jocelyn grinned and leaned over and tweaked his cheek. "Didn't want you to get any ideas, Steele."

An innocent look flashed across Bas's face before he gave her a warm smile. "You think I'd do something like that?"

"I'm not sure and I decided not to take any chances. This is supposed to be a fun weekend. Our definitions of fun might be vastly different."

His smile widened as he recalled the kisses that had flooded his mind all week. He just couldn't shake the memory of how her lips had felt beneath his, the taste of her, how their tongues had mingled, chased each other back and forth. "Oh, I think our definitions might be the same."

"You think so? Then how about telling me what you have planned for us next?"

Bas glanced over at her when he came to a stop sign. "I want to take you home with me."

She lifted a brow. "Excuse me?"

He smiled. "My family is giving my youngest brother Donovan a party for his thirty-first birthday next month and I'd like you to go with me."

"To your family's function?"

"Yes, as my guest."

A tiny flush warmed her cheeks. In the good old days when a man took a woman home to meet his family it meant something, but she knew that in this day and age of modern dating, the rules had changed and so had the expectations. You no longer needed a formal date to become romantically involved. The two of you could just meet somewhere and get it on. She'd even heard of the concept of video mobile dating. It seemed "try before you buy" was the way to go now.

"How will your family handle something like that?" she couldn't help but ask.

He grinned over at her before easing the car onto the interstate. "Seeing you will raise a few brows, I'm sure. I haven't seriously dated since I ended my engagement eight months ago."

She was about to tell him that he wasn't seriously dating now when the last part of his sentence stopped her. "You were engaged?" she asked, trying to stop her head from reeling and her eyes from spinning.

"Yes. You sound shocked. Don't you think I'm marriage material?"

She shrugged her shoulders. "For some reason I can't see you sitting by the fireplace with a pipe in your mouth while reading to the kiddies."

"Get rid of the pipe and go with the scene. I love kids and want a couple of them one day, and when I do settle down and marry, I plan to give my wife and children my absolute attention."

"Really. Then, what happened?"

"Let's just say Cassandra and I determined we weren't compatible after all," he said easily. Too easily for Jocelyn's way of thinking.

"How long were the two of you engaged?"

"Six months."

"And how long did the two of you date before becoming engaged?"

"Almost a year."

"Jeez, it took you that long to discover the two of you didn't fit? You don't come across to me as slow, Bas."

He didn't know whether to take her comment as a compliment or an insult. He chose the latter. "I'm not slow and there were reasons I hung in there for as long as I did."

Jocelyn sighed softly, wondering if love had been the reason. Had he loved this Cassandra person so much that he'd been determined to make things work between them? Did he still love her? "Do you think the two of you will ever work things out and get back together?"

"Excuse my French, but hell no. There's no way I'd consider such a thing."

Brushing her hair back from her eyes, Jocelyn glanced over at him. He certainly didn't sound like a man who was still in love. But then she was comparing him with Reese. Although Reese was bitter and angry with Leah, Jocelyn could still detect the deep love in his voice whenever he spoke about her sister. With Bas just now, all she heard was disgust.

"So, will you go home with me to Donovan's party, Jocelyn?"

She wasn't ready to give him her answer yet. "I'll let you know. And thanks for offering to do the driving," she added, feeling the need to change the subject.

"No problem. Just put your head back and relax. I'll have you in Memphis before you know it."

She smiled and tilted her seat back. "Just stay within the speed limit. I'm not sharing the cost of a ticket with you."

Bas chuckled. "You are the last person to give someone advice about speeding."

A small giggle slipped from Jocelyn's lips as she closed her eyes.

The hotel Jocelyn had chosen was right in the thick of things and as soon as they dropped their overnight bags off at their respective rooms, they met downstairs in the lobby, ready to explore, enjoy and have fun.

Memphis was known for its food, entertainment and hot spots. But this particular weekend it was all about jazz. What had begun a few years ago as an outdoor concert was now a full weekend of numerous blues and jazz events.

As if it was the most natural thing to do, Bas and Jocelyn wandered the streets holding hands as they shared meals and listened to music from jazz greats as well as students from the University of Memphis music department. One concert displayed a variety of cultures with the native music of the Caribbean, the Middle East and the rich musical heritage of the African-American culture blended together in a way that was soul-stirring at its best.

With vendors on each side the streets were narrow, and more than once Bas had to pull Jocelyn closer to his side to let others pass. Each time his hand touched her waist she would gaze up into the depths of his chocolate eyes and could only smile as an unnerving degree of heat slithered down her spine. Whenever she looked at him her thoughts wandered into forbidden territory and her mind was actually whirling with possibilities of how their night would end.

She clutched the bag filled with the purchases they had made, determined not to go there. Tonight she would go to her room and Bas would go to his; it was that simple. But a warm blush crept into her cheeks when she admitted that that likely wouldn't be the outcome at all. Something was happening to her. With very little effort Bas was doing something no other man had done—awakening her deepest desires. He was connecting to a part of her she had long denied existed. She inhaled deeply. Where was all that poise, self-control and composure she'd always prided herself on?

It was past midnight when they called it a day and began walking back toward their hotel, still holding hands. She recalled they'd even held hands throughout all the concerts they had attended.

"Did you have fun today?" she asked as they walked lazily through the streets. The crowd on the sidewalks had thinned out a lot. It was evident the people passing them by were party animals, still in a festive mood on their way to some nightclub or other.

Bas smiled at her. "Yes. This is the most fun I've had in a long time."

She grinned and leaned in closer to him. "Even more fun than the fishing trip last weekend?"

He chuckled. "This was a different sort of fun. I hadn't realized how much I've missed by not going to a jazz concert. CDs are nice but there's nothing like being right there in the audience, having the strings of a guitar and the melodic tune of a piano slowly hum through you. The vitality of it was awesome. Thanks for suggesting that we come."

She smiled, pleased. "You're welcome. I'm glad you enjoyed yourself."

When they reached the entrance to the hotel he suddenly stopped, turned toward her and slid his arms loosely around her neck. He leaned in closer, his mouth barely an inch from hers. "In fact, I may have had too much fun. I'm not ready for the night to end. Feel it?"

"Feel what?" The only thing she felt at that moment was the slow sizzle in her blood from the way he was looking at her. He was so close she could see the dark rings around his pupils, and that look made a deep-rooted longing uncurl inside her.

"Night heat."

She swallowed against the thickness that suddenly settled in her throat. "Night heat?"

"Yes. Maybe it's the sound of all that jazz, being surrounded by it while it works inexplicable sensations all through you. But I honestly think it's something else."

"What?"

"You. Me. Here. The night. The heat. The connection," he breathed against her lips. "Close your eyes and feel it."

Jocelyn closed her eyes and she began to feel it. She mentally savored the sounds around her, the conversations in the distance, the jazzy music that wasn't ready to end and the breathy sigh that escaped from between her own lips.

A sultry breeze made her sniff the air and she

took in the smell of Cajun food, spicy barbecue ribs, the steamy aroma of blue crabs. Then there was the scent of man, at least of the man standing in front of her. Of all the things she had taken in, he was the one thing that made the night steamy. Hot. He was everything she imagined night heat was about—a male rich in sensuality, masculinity and irresistible charm. A man who could make her heart pound from just one heated look. A man who gazed at you as though he was a predator and you were the object of his intent. "Yes, I can feel it," she murmured truthfully, before opening her eyes.

Her senses were jolted with the sudden feel of his mouth on hers. Hot and quick. His tongue captured hers before she could take her next breath and then just as quickly, he pulled away.

"There's a nightclub in the hotel. Do you want to go dancing?"

Jocelyn suddenly felt light-headed, dazed. The air surrounding them flickered softly across her skin, adding to the odd feeling she was experiencing. And at that moment she knew she too wasn't ready for the night to end. Trembling with a mixture of sensuality and excitement, she met his gaze, smiled and whispered, "Yes, I want to go dancing."

A deep tremor passed through Bas the moment he took Jocelyn into his arms on the dance floor. The air surrounding them was thick. The jazzy music encircling them was rich and smooth, and she was soft.

If she had been any other woman he would have suggested that they go up to his room instead of going dancing. Holding her against him, moving his body with hers to the sway of the music only intensified the temptation he was trying like hell to fight. He had been feeling something practically all day, but it had become more prevalent when night had set in. He wanted her to feel it, as well. He wanted her to acknowledge its existence as he had. From the first, this heat between them had been there. That was the reason he couldn't forget her kisses and the reason he wanted to hold her here now, sliding his body intimately against hers, wanting her to feel his desire, his longing, his want. He wanted to touch her all over and had to steady his hands, force them to remain at her back, stroking, caressing, although they were desperate to do more.

But he couldn't stop his lips from wanting to taste her, so he brushed them against hers, lightly, building passion one degree at a time. He doubted that he would ever get tired of kissing her, whether the kisses were light and breezy or deep and demanding. As he continued to delight her mouth with slow, easy kisses, he felt her body become almost weightless in his arms. He wanted to sweep her off her feet, into his embrace and take her to his room or hers to give her pleasure so intense she would remember this night for the rest of her life.

Damn. Something was happening to him. Emotions he was known to keep bottled up inside of him were fighting to seep out. In the past he'd been too busy plowing himself with work, but lately he'd had a lot of undemanding time to think and appreciate, to begin to enjoy life. And he was beginning to like having free time on his hands. He was enjoying having fun, leaving work on time and going to the gym and going fishing with Reese and his brothers. He couldn't recall the last time he had allowed himself the time to indulge in such simple pleasures.

After that summer with Jim, when he had returned home to finish college and work in the family business, he had placed himself on a rigid schedule that he'd gotten addicted to over the years. But now it seemed that Jocelyn Mason intended him to incorporate some fun into his life, and he was actually looking forward to it. He was even eager to settle down and start working on that paint-by-number kit she had talked him into purchasing today from one of the sidewalk vendors. It was a picture of a woodland chalet with snowcapped mountains in the background, a scene that reminded him of Newton Grove. He was excited to get started on it. More than anything, he'd enjoyed taking the time off this weekend to spend with Jocelyn.

The breath rushed out of him when he realized he was beginning to feel something for the woman he held so close to him. She had the ability to fire a need within him that he hadn't felt in years, if ever. And it wasn't all sexual, although he did have this vivid mental image in his mind of how wonderful it would be to have her in his bed to play out all those fantasies and dreams he'd had of her lately. Thinking about them only made him want her more. Being here with her, dancing with her, holding her in his arms while her cheek rested on his chest, seemed as natural as breathing, and a satisfying sensation skittered all the way down his belly.

"Bas?"

He barely heard her whisper his name. "Yes?"

"Can we go somewhere else?"

Her request heated the desire he felt through his entire body. "Where do you want to go?"

"You decide."

And with a low growl, he did. He took her hand in his and led her off the dance floor and out of the nightclub to a place where they could finish what they had started.

"You're beautiful."

Bas whispered the words the moment he stepped into Jocelyn's hotel room and swept her into his arms. The heat that had been simmering within her all day had escalated during the ride in the elevator and what seemed like a long, endless walk down the hall to her room.

"If I'm beautiful, then you are, too," she said truthfully. There was just something about him that stirred her blood, awakened desires within her and sent rushes of heat thrumming all through her.

Jocelyn had stopped fighting the feeling and was willing to surrender to the inevitable. Since that day in Jason's office the attraction had been great, bigger, it seemed, than both of them. She hadn't planned for anything to happen between them this weekend; it was to be fun on her terms. She had gone through life without intimacy with a man, and she assumed she could certainly go on in the same way a while longer. But hadn't Bas warned her about assuming anything?

"Let's dispense with all the compliments," he said, moving toward the sofa instead of the bed. He saw her confused look and gave her a sexy smile that touched her all the way to her toes. After he'd sat down with her cuddled in his arms he said, "I won't go that far until I'm certain our definitions are the same, Jocelyn."

She frowned. "They are," she said, her voice raw and thick.

"I've got to be sure it's not just the night."

Her frown deepened. It *was* the night but that wasn't all it was. "I don't understand."

"When you wake up in the morning I don't want you to have any regrets."

"And you think I will?"

"Not sure. All I know is that when you left Newton Grove this morning you had no intentions of sleeping with me."

"Can't a girl change her mind?"

"Yes, but I have to know it's for the right reason. I won't assume anything."

He saw the flicker of disappointment in her eyes and his lips curved into a seductive smile. "If only you knew how much I want you, how much I want to be inside you, take you with every breath in my body, while replaying every dream I've had of you since the first day I laid eyes on you, you'd know how much not making love to you is killing me."

"It doesn't look like you're dying to me," she said with a bit of sting in her voice as she broke eye contact with him. She just couldn't figure men out. They wanted you when you weren't willing and didn't want you when you were.

As if he read her thoughts he reached out and placed a finger at her chin to lift her gaze back to his. "This is not a game I'm playing, Jocelyn. I want you so much I hurt, and to show you just how much, I'm going to leave you with something to remember me by tonight."

And then he kissed her with a demand that had her

body shuddering all at once. He entered her mouth with a force that claimed it as his, totally, irrevocably. She felt him shift her body in his lap and ease the jacket from her shoulders while not breaking contact with her lips. And then his hands were on her, caressing her through her blouse, and then slipping his fingers beneath it to cup her breasts. He slowly stroked his thumb in the center, across her bra-clad nipple and captured in his mouth the ragged sigh that escaped from deep within her throat.

He eased his mouth from hers. "I want to taste you all over," he murmured. "I've been fantasizing about doing it since the first time I kissed you. You have a unique taste that drives me wild. It makes me want to savor every single inch of you."

Before Jocelyn could pull in her next breath Bas brought her to her feet to face him and in seconds he was pulling her blouse over her head, then tossing it aside to join her jacket. He released her long enough to slide the jacket off his shoulders and throw it aside, as well.

He took one look at her, standing in front of him in her black lace bra, before leaning over and covering his mouth with hers once again. Sexual sparks crackled, tore into her when she felt his fingers release the clasp of her bra, and then he broke the kiss long enough to strip it off her.

"I've got to taste you here," he whispered, seconds

before capturing her around the waist and lowering his face to her chest. His mouth immediately latched on her breasts, kissed them until her nipples ached. He knew exactly how to flicker the tip of his tongue across them, lave them in a circle motion that drove her wild, made her panties wet. She was grateful for the strong, solid arms holding her upright or else she would have crumpled to the floor from the shockwaves that were tearing through her.

He slowly pulled back, got down on his knees and began working at the snap of her jeans. He glanced up, held her gaze while he eased the denim down her hips, pausing to help her step out of her shoes before taking the jeans completely off her and tossing them aside, leaving her standing in front of him in just a pair of black lacy boxer-style undies.

He leaned back on his haunches, and she wondered if he had changed his mind after all. Seconds later she knew he hadn't when he reached out and slowly eased her panties down her hips, inhaling deeply while doing so.

"You smell good," he said in a tone filled with so much desire it made her body tremble. He leaned forward, held her gaze and whispered, "I need to taste you. Now."

He trailed hot, wet kisses across her belly before moving lower, and with the palms of his hands he gently eased her legs apart. Jocelyn stopped breathing, anticipating his next move. He didn't disappoint her. He leaned closer and gripped her hips, then buried his face in her. When he slipped that same hot, wet tongue inside her, she released a moan that came from so deep in her throat she actually felt her knees buckle beneath her.

But his solid grip held her in place while his mouth made love to her, tasting, devouring, feasting. He was unashamedly greedy, intent on getting his fill, making her dig her nails into his shoulders. Unable to control the shudders racking her, she threw her head back and forced air through her lungs before screaming out his name.

"Bas!"

Her entire body shook, came apart with the force of the climax. Never had she encountered such a fierce, powerful reaction, an earth-shattering explosion. She held his shoulders tight and writhed helplessly against him, while his tongue did things to her no other man had ever done.

And as she continued to soar to a place she had never been before, she knew that Sebastian Steele was more than a troubleshooter and a problem solver. He was the epitome of what female fantasies were made of. He was temptation at its finest, a man who delivered with action, a man with one incredible mouth, a man who knew just how to pleasure a woman.

And at that moment, while aftershocks slithered

down her spine, she was blinded by the staggering realization that if she didn't stop herself, she could fall deliriously and passionately in love with him.

"Umm." With a deep, satisfying moan Jocelyn shifted her body in bed as delicious dreams continued to filter through her sleep-induced mind. Strong, firm hands parted her thighs, and the urgency that filled her with profound emotions made her body brace for a joining she needed, one she craved and one that had every inch of her braced in anticipation for—

The sharp ringing of the phone had her bolting upright. She rubbed her hand across her face and snatched up the phone then hung it back up. It had merely been the hotel's wake-up call.

She settled back in bed and remembered her dream. Some of it had been a dream and some of it reality. She closed her eyes, remembering the part that had been real, and the memory wrenched a serious moan through her lips. Bas had kissed her all over, devoured her, made her come, then he'd picked her up, carried her over to the bed and tucked her in. Before leaving, he had kissed her, sending shudders through her body long after he'd left. And then she had drifted off to sleep, only to finalize in her dreams what he had refused to do during her wakeful moments.

Still, she felt wonderful.

Sighing deeply, she forced herself up in bed again and ran her fingers through her hair. They were supposed to meet downstairs for an early breakfast before heading back to Newton Grove. How was she supposed to face him knowing what he had done to her last night? What she had let him do? But she had no regrets. The pleasure she still felt was too intense for her to be repentant. He had wanted her and she had wanted him; yet he had maintained his control, assumed nothing and had given her pleasure while withholding his own.

As she slipped out of bed she released a long-drawn-out sigh. Aftershocks of passion surged through every part of her body. Her blood felt hot, her body hotter and more than anything she wanted him to finish what he'd started. But she'd get her chance this coming weekend to prove that although neither of them should assume anything, some things were a gimme. What Leah had said a couple of weeks ago was right: when Bas finished what he came to do he would be gone. There was nothing to hold him in Newton Grove, and she had to remember that.

But for now she wanted to enjoy whatever he was offering, and when he did leave she wouldn't have any regrets.

Chapter 12

Leah glanced up from her book when she heard the sound of a drill outside the house. Pushing out of the chair, she crossed to the window and gasped when a man's face came into view.

Reese!

She clutched her chest, wondering what on earth he was doing outside her window. Not *her* window exactly. She had driven over to Jocelyn's house to finish doing laundry when her dad's washing machine had suddenly gone on the blink.

Reese had seen her through the window at the same time she'd seen him and through the glass she could read his expression. His frown spoke volumes. He wasn't happy at seeing her and within minutes he had made his way to the front door and was knocking hard.

She crossed the room and snatched it open. "What are you doing here, Reese?"

He narrowed his eyes at her. "I could ask you the same thing."

She decided biting each other's heads off wouldn't accomplish anything so she said as calmly as she could, "Jocelyn went away for the weekend and when Dad's washing machine broke down I decided to come over here and use hers. And I thought she mentioned that you and your brother were going to the races in Kentucky this weekend."

He leaned in the doorway, apparently annoyed. "Little Danny got sick so Daniel wanted to hang around."

"Is little Danny okay?"

He resented hearing the concern in her voice. "Yes, it's just a stomach virus but Rita almost went bonkers because he's rarely sick. Since the trip was cancelled I decided to fix that floodlight outside that's been giving Jocelyn trouble."

"Oh. Then don't let me keep you." She was about to shut the door when he stuck his foot out, halting it from closing.

"You think you can just dismiss me like that?

After all these years don't you think you owe me some type of explanation, Leah?" he asked angrily.

Leah breathed in sharply. Coming face to face with Reese again a little more than a week after their first encounter wasn't good. There was nothing she could tell him, nothing she could say to make things right, so it was best not to say anything at all. "No, I don't owe you an explanation."

She made an attempt to close the door on him again, but in anger he shoved it open. She took a step back when he stormed in and slammed it shut behind him. "The hell you don't," he roared as if all the anger he'd been holding inside him had suddenly snapped.

"Have you lost your mind, Reese?"

"I lost my mind years ago since I must have been crazy to get mixed up with the likes of you in the first place," he said, anger seeping out of his every pore. "You are one ungrateful, selfish, self-centered human being."

"Get out!"

"Make me. I won't leave until I've had my say."

"I won't listen." She turned away and walked toward the kitchen.

He was right on her heels. "Oh, you'll listen. When I think of all the time and love I put into this place for you and for you to treat me like dirt and—"

She turned around, almost coming nose to nose

with him. She stared at him in shock. "What are you talking about?"

"This house, damn you, was supposed to be ours. I built it for you and was going to surprise you with it on your birthday but you hauled ass. You left without looking back, letting me know I was nothing more to you than a trinket to play with. You cared nothing for me. All your words of love were nothing but lies!"

Leah went completely still, frozen in place. She blinked her dazed eyes. "What do you mean you built this house for me?"

"Look around, Leah. This house has everything you always said you wanted in a home. I built it with my own hands for you. I worked with your dad during the day and worked here late at night, some-times past midnight, and on weekends, sometimes tired to the bone, just to give you what you wanted, or what you claimed you wanted—a place to live with me as my wife, to raise our children. But you never meant any of it."

His words were too much. She hadn't known. No one had ever told her about the house. How could Jocelyn and her father not tell her? Just as the hold on his temper had broken earlier, so did the flood-gates of pain she had held within her for five years. She wanted to scream and fisted her hand into her mouth to stop from doing so, but that didn't stop the fierce tremors that racked her body.

"What the hell's wrong with you, Leah?"

Reese's temper cleared enough for him to see that something strange was happening to Leah. It was as if all the coloring had left her face and she was shaking. He reached out and touched her and she pulled back from his touch. She resembled a creature gone wild and began backing away from him, looking at him as if she didn't know who he was. She had a crazed look in her eyes. He took a step toward her. "Leah, what's wrong?"

"No, don't touch me again. Don't come near me. No! No! Please no."

He swore and took a step toward her, concerned. "What's the matter with you, Leah? Tell me what's wrong. Why are you looking at me that way? I wouldn't hurt you, you know that."

"No! Don't come near me. Don't you dare touch me again. I belong to Reese and you can't do that to me. I won't let you. I hate you!"

Reese wasn't entirely sure what was going on here but he knew Leah had gone into some kind of shock, as if she was reliving something bad that had happened. The thought of what that could be was like a punch in his stomach.

"Who do you think I am, Leah?" he asked quietly, deciding to use another approach. "Who do you think I am?"

"I know who you are, Neil. And I won't let you hurt me again. You won't ever force yourself on me again."

Neil? Reese frowned. The only Neil he knew was Neil Grunthall, but the man was dead. In fact, come to think of it, he had died around the same time Leah had disappeared. His eyes flamed as a thought entered his mind. It was one he didn't want to consider but was forced to, knowing what a bastard Neil Grunthall had been and how the man had hated his guts. "Did Neil touch you?" he asked with deadly calm.

It was as if she hadn't heard him. She kept backing up and when he walked toward her she picked up a vase off Jocelyn's coffee table and held it high like a weapon, ready to throw it at a moment's notice. "You come near me and I'll kill you. I couldn't defend myself before but I can now."

"Oh, Leah." Her words, spoken in such a heart-wrenching and tortured tone, broke everything inside of Reese and there was no way he could not go to her at that moment.

"No! I said not to come near me!"

When he got close she made good on her threat and threw the vase at him. He ducked out of the way, and it shattered on the hardwood floor. The sound made her jerk and that was all the time Reese needed to close in and grab her.

"No, Neil, let me go!" she cried out. "I belong to Reese. Don't do this. Don't hurt me again. I love Reese. Please let me go!"

She fought him, kicked and bit the knuckle on his left hand, but his arms wrapped around her like steel beams, refusing to let her hurt him or herself. "It's okay, baby. I'm Reese and you do belong to me," he whispered quietly against her struggles. "Neil is dead, Leah, and he won't hurt you again. He won't hurt you again."

He said the words over and over before he finally began getting through to her. When he did, she broke down and began crying in earnest. The tortured sound, similar to the sound of a wounded animal, tore at his heart and brought tears to his eyes. "It's okay, baby. It's okay."

When she went limp he picked her up and walked over to Jocelyn's spare bedroom. Shoving open the door with his shoulder, he carried her over to the bed and placed her there.

He drew back and gazed down at her. She refused to open her eyes and look at him. "Leah," he said gently, "rest and we'll talk."

She turned away from him and faced the wall. "No, please leave," she said quietly, sounding defeated, humiliated and embarrassed. "I want to be alone."

Her words tugged at his heart. There was no way in hell he would leave her alone. He remembered Jocelyn saying that she would be returning to town around noon that day and he intended to stay put until she got there. "I'm not leaving, Leah. I'll be in the living room if you need me. Try and get some rest."

He then turned and walked out of the room, quietly closing the door behind him.

When the car came to a traffic light Bas glanced over at Jocelyn. They were about to get on the interstate to head back to Newton Grove. She had the seat reclined to a comfortable position and was resting with her eyes closed. At least he thought they were closed but he couldn't tell beneath the dark sunglasses.

During breakfast she hadn't had a whole lot to say and had avoided discussing what they'd shared last night. But with all the memories flooding his mind, he couldn't think of anything else.

She looked different this morning. More rested and relaxed. Her hair fell in glossy curls around her shoulders and the lime green of her skirt and matching sweater made her dark coloring that much more beautiful. He remembered last night and how she'd stood there while he'd loved her with his mouth. He hadn't regretted anything about what he'd done and wondered if she had. There was only one way to find out.

"You okay?" he asked quietly.

She glanced over at him and smiled. "Yes. Is there any reason why I wouldn't be?"

He shrugged. "You've been quiet this morning."

She sighed and stared ahead. "I've been thinking."

"Oh. You want to share your thoughts?"

She glanced back over at him. "I was wondering how to convey my thanks to you for giving me something really special last night."

He felt a rush of pleasure that she didn't have any regrets about what they'd shared. "Conveying your thanks isn't necessary because you gave me something special, as well."

She raised her brow. "What?"

"A chance to savor a special part of you."

Heat sizzled her skin and a yearning erupted in the pit of her stomach when she thought of how he had done so. "Yes, but you took things a step further when you exposed me to your incredible experience and masterful skills."

He chuckled. "Did I do that?"

She angled her face toward him. "Yes, you did." Moments later she said, "And I've decided to go to your brother's party with you after all."

He smiled then, pleased with her decision. He glanced over at her when the car came to a stop at another traffic light. He wished she didn't have her sunglasses on because he wanted to look into the depths of her dark eyes, see if they held some clue as to why she'd made that decision.

"Why are you staring at me like that?"

"Mmm, I was just thinking that you have such a pretty face."

She laughed. "Thanks, and if you keep saying such nice things, I might want to keep you around."

He grinned. "That's what I'm hoping."

An angry Reese paced Jocelyn's living room, getting angrier by the second. Why hadn't anyone told him what had happened to Leah? How could they keep something like that from him? And to think that for five solid years he had hated her, despised her, tried to eradicate her from his memory…his heart.

The scene that had played out in this very living room less than an hour ago had his stomach in knots. Neil Grunthall had forced himself on Leah! The thought of her defenseless against Neil made Reese's entire body shake in rage.

He sighed, trying to recall what Jocelyn had almost let slip the other day when she'd come to Leah's defense. She was certain her sister wasn't pregnant because, according to Jocelyn, he was the last man Leah had been involved with. What she hadn't said was that someone had forced himself on her.

He doubted he would forget for as long as he lived the crazed look in Leah's eyes when he had touched her. Hell, he could just imagine what had played out in her mind. He'd watched a special episode on rape victims on CNN once and according to the reporter, some women never fully recovered from such an ordeal and were encouraged to seek some type of professional counseling. He wondered if Leah had done so.

Had that been the reason she had left town all those years ago, he wondered. Considering the timing of everything, a part of him knew that it had been. Why hadn't she come to him and told him what had happened? It would have given him sheer pleasure to kill Neil Grunthall with his bare hands. If the man wasn't already dead, there was no way he would be living now.

But hating Neil wouldn't undo what he'd done to Leah. The woman he loved was now his main concern and yes, he loved her. He had never stopped loving her and he vowed then that if her spirit was still broken from all of this, he intended to repair it.

More than anything he wanted Leah to know he would always be there for her, no matter what.

Pleased that Jocelyn had no regrets about last night, Bas set his mind on getting them back to Newton Grove. She had mentioned a baby shower for a friend she wanted to attend that afternoon.

He picked up the cup of coffee and took a sip, appreciating the taste, and smiled when he thought of another taste he appreciated—the one belonging to the woman sitting beside him who had dozed off to sleep. With the windows up, her luscious scent filled the confines of the car and he couldn't stop the desire that quickly encircled his gut. It was difficult to recall the last time he'd wanted a woman so much.

He tried to rationalize his attraction to her. She was a beautiful woman but he had met beautiful women before. What was there about Jocelyn that made him feel emotions he'd never felt before? In his book she was P and P: proper and passionate.

He'd seen her proper side one evening when she hadn't been aware she was being observed. It had been a social ball a couple of weeks ago that Ms. Sadie's group of older ladies had given for some debutantes. Sadie hadn't been able to get her car started and when he'd come in from a workout at the gym, she had asked if he would drop her off. He had pulled up in front of the Civic Center in time to see a very sophisticated-looking Jocelyn meet and greet all the other guests. She hadn't seen him, but he had seen her and what he'd called her proper side.

He smiled, knowing that beneath that proper side was a passionate side, one yet to be explored to the fullest. She was definitely a woman who could make his blood run hot. She was a distraction but a distraction that he liked.

It suddenly hit him why he felt that way, and emotions he'd tried analyzing for the past couple of weeks instantly became crystal-clear. He was falling in love with Jocelyn. And if he wasn't careful, she could become the person he loved more than anyone in his entire life.

But that thought didn't bother him and he hoped to hell it didn't bother her when she discovered how he felt. He wouldn't shock her by declaring his affections, at least not now. He wanted them to spend more time together, to have what she considered fun, before he broached such a serious subject with her. He had discovered that Jocelyn didn't handle surprises very well.

"If you've done a thorough review of the company books, then I guess you know that my dad and Noreen were having an affair."

Her words, spoken out of the blue, surprised the hell out of Bas. He jerked his head and stared at her. He thought she was sleeping. "You knew?"

She smiled. "Yes, even though they thought I didn't. Believe me, they were very discreet, but there were some things you couldn't help but notice—like the looks they gave each other when they thought no one else was around."

"Did you have a problem with it?"

Jocelyn shrugged. "I did at first. No girl wants to imagine her parent being sexually active, but then I saw how happy he was, and what a great mood he was in whenever he returned from one of his mystery trips out of town."

She chuckled. "After spending a weekend out of town with you I have an idea of just how he felt."

An hour later, after arriving back in Newton Grove, Bas was driving them through the city. "Do you want me to take you home or to your father's house?" he asked, glancing over at Jocelyn when he came to a stop at a traffic light. She looked refreshed from her nap, and the desire he'd been holding at bay suddenly kicked into high gear. Combined with the love he felt for her, the emotion completely overwhelmed him.

"You can take me on home and I—"

Before she finished whatever she was about to say, Bas leaned over and brought his mouth down on hers, effectively snatching both breath and words from her throat. She responded and when his tongue darted into her mouth, she captured it with her own, sucked on it before he could pull back.

When he straightened up in his seat, he smiled at her. "You're coming up with some pretty masterful skills yourself."

She chuckled as she raked her fingers through her hair. "Only because I have a good teacher. I was just following his lead."

Bas's pulse rate increased and he couldn't wait until he got to her place. His goodbye kiss would be one she remembered for a long time. Well, maybe not, he thought moments later when he pulled into her driveway and saw the two vehicles parked there. She had left her car for her sister to use and he recognized the truck as Reese's.

"Looks like you have company."

Jocelyn glanced up. When she saw the two vehicles, a deep frown settled on her face. "Oh, no," she said, unsnapping her seat belt before Bas brought the car to a stop. "What are the two of them doing here together?"

Her question, as well as the worried expression on her face, confused Bas. "Maybe they're trying to patch things up."

Jocelyn shook her head. "It won't be that easy."

He lifted a brow. "Why?"

"Because it won't. Please stop the car, Bas."

Upon hearing the panic in her voice, he stopped the car and the minute he did she threw open the door and raced toward her house. Not knowing what the hell was going on, he took off after her.

Before she could use her key to open the door, it was snatched open and an angry Reese came out and glared at Jocelyn. "Dammit why didn't you tell me, Joce?"

She didn't answer. Instead she tried to move past him to go into the house. "Where's Leah?"

He blocked her path. "She's asleep, but I want to know why you didn't tell me."

"Not now Reese, I have to—"

"No! I want to know why you didn't tell me."

Bas heard the anger in Reese's voice, anger that was directed at Jocelyn. He also noted that Reese was blocking the way into her own house. Bas stepped forward. "Calm down, Reese. What's going on? What has you so upset? Is something wrong with Leah?"

Reese's glare left Jocelyn and moved to Bas. "Yeah, something is wrong with her all right, something I didn't know about until today."

He then moved his gaze back to Jocelyn. The eyes that looked at her were filled with a mixture of rage and anguish. "My God, Jocelyn, why didn't you tell me that Neil Grunthall had raped her?"

Chapter 13

Jocelyn's eyes widened. "Leah actually told you?"

Having his suspicions confirmed was like a kick in Reese's gut, and it took everything he had not to ram his fist into the nearest post. "She didn't tell me willingly," he said with fury lining his every word. "I confronted her about why she left and when I told her about this house she started shaking uncontrollably. I reached out to calm her down, and when I did all hell broke loose. She went berserk as if she was reliving those moments with Neil and actually thought I was him."

Reese paused long enough to rub a tortured hand

down his face. The eyes that looked at Jocelyn again were hard and angrier than before. "Why didn't you or your dad tell me?"

Jocelyn inhaled deeply, hearing the hurt, pain and despair in his voice. "Dad never knew and I only found out myself a few weeks ago, Reese," she said softly. "And she made me promise not to tell you."

Reese's head fell back against the wooden post and he looked up at the sky as if the clouds held some kind of comfort for him. Then he looked back at Jocelyn. "Tell me what happened. Please. I need to know."

Jocelyn slid her gaze from Reese to Bas. He was staring at her just as intently as Reese, although he hadn't said anything. She knew Leah was still in love with Reese just as Reese was still in love with Leah. If anyone could break through the barriers Leah had erected, it would be Reese.

"All right," she said wearily. "But I want you to promise you'll be patient and understanding and—"

"My God, Joce, of course I'll be patient and understanding. I love Leah," he said in a tortured moan. "I've never stopped loving her even when I thought she had done me wrong. If you think I'll turn my back on her now, knowing what she's been through, then you don't know me."

Jocelyn inhaled deeply. She did know him and she

knew how much he loved her sister. Somehow, through it all, his heart had remained intact even when his mind had assumed the worst.

Assumed.

She shook her head. Bas had helped her to see how that one little word could cause a world of trouble. "Okay, I'll tell you what she told me."

"On that note I think I'll wait out in the car," Bas said, turning to leave, thinking he'd heard more than he should have already. This was a private matter between Jocelyn, Reese and Leah.

"No, please stay, Bas," Jocelyn said, not understanding why but knowing she needed him there.

Bas turned back around and met the silent plea in her gaze and knew at that moment he could deny her nothing.

He glanced over at Reese. "You're okay with me staying?"

Reese nodded. "Yeah, man. I'm okay with it."

Moments later, after telling the two men everything, Jocelyn shifted her gaze from Reese. It was hard not to see the tears that filled his eyes without getting misty-eyed, as well.

And then there was Bas. She had seen him ball his fist in anger several times, and although he hadn't said anything, the tightening of his jaw and the fury that lined his eyes had said it all.

"Did she get any professional help?" Reese asked, breaking the silence.

"Yes, but there are still issues she's trying to work through, hurdles she's yet to cross. It takes time recovering from an ordeal such as that."

"No matter how long it takes, I'm going to be there with her," Reese said in a firm voice. "We're going to work through this thing, Leah and I. Together."

Jocelyn smiled. "She's not going to make things easy for you, Reese. Already she's talking about returning to California in a few weeks."

Reese nodded, and although he didn't say anything, Jocelyn knew he had no intentions of letting Leah go anywhere. "She's sleeping now, but I want to be there when she wakes up, to talk to her, Jocelyn. Alone."

Jocelyn knew what he was asking of her. The mothering instinct in her demanded that she see to her sister herself, but she knew Reese was right. He was the one who needed to be there for Leah. "Okay." She then glanced over at Bas. "Do you want to go grab some lunch?"

Bas smiled. She had a feeling he agreed wholeheartedly with her decision to let Reese handle Leah in his own way. "Yes, lunch sounds good and I know just where I want to take you."

Leah came awake, remembering where she was. Then she recalled her argument with Reese and…

"Oh my God!" She covered her face with her hands when it all came tumbling back to her. He knew. There was no way he would not have figured things out.

"Are you okay?"

She jumped then turned in the bed to face Reese, her eyes going wide. He was standing in the doorway. "What are you doing here?"

"I told you I wasn't going anywhere, Leah. Besides, I think we should talk."

No! She didn't want to talk. She wanted to be as far away from him as she could. Knowing that he knew what had happened to her was too much. She quickly slipped off the bed. "I just want to finish my laundry and leave. Jocelyn should be back any minute and—"

"Jocelyn is already back. She and Bas went somewhere for lunch. They knew I wanted to talk to you alone."

"We have nothing to talk about."

He ignored her and took a step into the room, and she automatically backed up. Her seemingly frightened retreat almost broke Reese's heart. "Why didn't you tell me what Neil had done to you? Why did you run away instead? Didn't you think I had a right to know?"

"Why? So you could kill him with your bare hands and go to jail? He wasn't worth it, Reese. He was nothing but a troublemaker and I knew I couldn't tell you or my father. Besides," she said, lowering her voice, fighting back her tears, "he wasn't your problem."

He took another step into the room. "You were mine, Leah. I loved you. I was going to marry you. Your problems were my problems. We would have worked things out."

"No, I had to leave. I felt dirty. Used. I felt unworthy. Don't you understand how difficult it is for me now, knowing that you know?"

"You should have told me. It would have changed nothing."

Leah turned away from him, trying to block whatever emotional reactions she was having to his words. Why couldn't he understand that she couldn't tell him? At the time she had felt battered, bruised and confused.

"Leah, please don't shut me out. I love you. I always have. I still do."

She turned back around, her eyes filled to capacity with tears. His admission of love was the last thing she wanted to hear, the last thing she wanted to know. Knowing he loved her and that he'd built this house for her was too much. "No, we can't go there, Reese. We can't go back. Too much has happened. After I left and went to California, I had a hard time dealing with things. If a man looked at me, I panicked. Finally, I knew I needed help and sought out professional assistance. With the aid of counselors and a very special support group, I began to see that I wasn't alone. There were other women who'd been violated like I had. And then there was Grace, the older woman who was kind enough to give me a place to stay in her home. She became the mother I had lost, the grandmother I'd never had and the friend that I needed. I've come a long way but I still have a long way to go."

"And we'll go there together. I love you too much to let you leave me a second time."

The sincerity in his words touched her and nervously she placed her lower lip between her teeth and met his gaze. He was being honest with her, leaving her no choice but to be completely honest with him, as well. "And I love you, too, Reese. Too much for you to get involved and waste your time with me. The love I knew you had for me is what helped me keep my sanity over the years. But each time I came home I knew that love was turning to hate and I had to learn how to get stronger without your love as a crutch because it wasn't there anymore and I couldn't pretend that it was."

She wiped the tears from her eyes before continuing. "I still haven't gotten over things to the point where I trust men. In fact, the thought of one ever touching me makes me ill. Even you. Knowing that, how can I even consider us picking up where we left off?"

"Like I said, we'll work through—"

"No, there's nothing to work through. In a few weeks I'm returning to California. I'm going to use the money I'm getting from Jocelyn to open a small restaurant there. My life, the one I do have, is in California. There's nothing for me here."

"I'm here, Leah," he said quietly. "The man who loves you."

She shook her head. "No, I can't take what you're offering. I can't and I won't."

Not giving him a chance to say anything else, she walked around him and out of the room.

Jocelyn replaced her cell phone in her purse and glanced over at Bas when he brought the car to a stop at the traffic light. "That was Reese. Things didn't go with Leah the way he'd hoped, but he's determined to help her through this."

Bas nodded. "He loves her very much."

"Always has. At one time I actually envied what they shared, it was so special. And I've always known that if there was one person who could get Leah to change her mind about leaving Newton Grove it was going to be Reese, just like I truly believe he's the one person who can heal her hurt."

"I'm going to have to agree with you on that."

Jocelyn had been waiting to hear from Reese, and with the phone call from him out of the way, she took the time to study her surroundings out the car's window. Lifting a brow, she glanced back over at Bas. "I thought we were headed back to town for lunch. Where are we going?"

He smiled although he couldn't take his eyes off the road to look over at her. "My place. I'm treating you to lunch."

Jocelyn blinked. "Your place? I thought you were staying at Sadie's Bed and Breakfast."

"I was, until Friday. While I was out riding around with Reese a few weeks ago, I saw this cabin on the outskirts of town and thought it would be a nice piece of investment property for the Steele Corporation. All of us like to get away every once in a while and we all love the mountains. Our parents own a cabin that we use occasionally, but this one is bigger."

"So you bought it? Just like that?"

He risked glancing over at her before returning his eyes to the road. Just for that instant he felt his heart slam hard in his chest. He did love her. He was no longer falling in love with her; he had fallen—and hard.

"Yes, just like that," he said, feeling like a man on top of the world. He would feel even better if the woman who held his affections felt the same way, but he knew that she didn't. But he had time to spare, and pretty soon she would see that Reese wasn't the only man on a mission to win over the woman he loved.

"So what's for lunch?" she asked.

"I thought I'd keep it simple and fix a couple of sandwiches. I haven't had a chance to do any real grocery shopping yet, but I do have stuff to make a nice sandwich."

"What kind of sandwich?"

When he brought the car to a stop in front of his cabin, he cocked his head and shot her a smile that tilted the corners of his lips. "I hope you like peanut butter and jelly."

Jocelyn had to admit that the peanut butter and jelly sandwich and glass of iced tea were good. She hadn't eaten since breakfast so her hunger might have been what had made it so delicious. But then she thought of something else that was delicious, something she liked—Bas's kisses.

"What are you thinking about?"

"Oh." A blush stained her cheeks. She'd thought he was using the restroom. She hadn't known he'd returned and had been staring at her. "I—" She paused, wondering what she could say. "I was just thinking about Reese and Leah," she lied, figuring he would believe that.

"And the thought of them is what had you smiling?"

"Er…yeah," she said, compounding her lie. "I can remember happier times."

"Don't give up on them. The happier times will return."

"You think so?"

"Yes," he said without hesitation. "When two people love each other, things will work out for them."

She lifted a brow. "You sound like someone who knows."

He shook his head. "Trust me, I'm not, but I believe it, and I've seen it happen. Take my brother Chance and his wife, Kylie. They butted heads from the start, but finally they decided to give love a try and eventually got married. And I don't know two happier people."

Jocelyn nodded, glanced around. For a place that had been moved in to a mere three days ago, Bas's place looked lived in. The three-bedroom, two-bath two-story log cabin with cathedral ceilings, sat secluded on a stream with hardwood trees all around. It also had an extraordinary view of the mountains, a wood-burning fireplace and a covered porch with an outdoor hot tub.

"You still planning on going to that baby shower later?"

She turned, not knowing he had crossed the room and was standing so close. "No, I'm not in the mood," she said softly, barely realizing what she was saying. Being this close to Bas was as usual stirring her senses, all five of them.

There was the scent of him, strong and manly with a come-hither aroma that should be bottled.

The sight of him, especially in his jeans, was provocative enough to make a woman's mouth water... And speaking of mouth, the taste of him from last night was still on her tongue. Even the peanut butter hadn't been able to eradicate it. Her taste buds were sensitive, tingling, anticipating kissing him again. Just thinking about it was putting another sense to work—her hearing. She could hear the pounding of her heart against her chest.

And then there was the sense of touch, something she hadn't quite explored to the fullest when it came to him. A soft sigh escaped her lungs at the thought of touching him intimately, taking him in her hands, feeling him harden beneath her fingers.

"You're smiling again," he said, resting his hip against his kitchen counter. "Still thinking about Reese and Leah?"

Jocelyn chewed the inside of her cheek, wondering what his reaction would be if she told him what she'd really been thinking about. She swallowed, deciding not to chance it. So she told him something that wasn't a lie, but it wasn't the full truth, either. "I was thinking about this weekend."

Bas smiled. "Now isn't that a coincidence. So was I."

"And what was your favorite part?" she asked him, wondering if it was the same as hers.

He deliberately licked his lips and eased up closer

to her. "I can't believe you have to ask me that, sweetheart," he said in a low voice.

Heat suddenly seemed to bubble up in Jocelyn's throat. The sight of his tongue was sending unflagging warmth all through her. "You enjoyed that, huh?"

"Most definitely," he whispered, leaning in closer to her.

Jocelyn breathed in, remembering the nights she hadn't been able to sleep because of thoughts of him, and she knew there was something she wanted to know.

Something she *had* to know.

Last night she had had an orgasm standing up. She wondered how one felt lying down in a bed. A slow burn began building between her legs at the thought of finding out. And she knew she couldn't leave this cabin until she did.

A part of her knew that she and Bas would never be a real couple. His home was in North Carolina and hers was here. There was nothing to keep him in Newton Grove when it was time for him to leave. But there was something the two of them could share while he was here. It was something she had never shared with a man before. A hot and torrid love affair. It would all be in the name of fun. In the end there would be no hard feelings and no regrets.

She could do this. She wanted to do this. She *needed* to do this.

Bas had awakened feelings and urges within her that she'd never had to deal with before. Not only had he awakened them, he had stirred them up real good and hot. She knew if she wanted to take things to the next level it would be up to her to make the move. He probably assumed that if he made them, she would accuse him of moving too fast. Hadn't he told her about the problem with assuming things?

Making the decision to take matters into her own hands, she smiled and pointed past him. "Have you used your fireplace yet?"

He glanced over his shoulder and then back at her. "No, why, are you cold?"

"No, I'm not cold." She sighed deeply. For God's sake, she told herself, don't lose your nerve now. Remember that article you read in *Today's Black Woman*? Sometimes it's up to you to let a man know what you want, Jocelyn Isabella Mason. She smiled, thinking that although she wasn't named after her father, together her initials spelled JIM.

"But I think a fire would be nice," she decided to say. She wanted this man and she intended to have him, for whatever time she could.

"Okay. Just make yourself comfortable."

"Thanks, I will," she said walking over to the sofa and taking a seat.

It didn't take Bas any time at all to get the fire started, mainly because one had already started to flame, right in his gut. He wasn't born yesterday. He could recognize seduction a mile away. But in this case it wasn't a mile away, it was right smack in his living room and sitting on his sofa.

He stood and turned around and the flame in his gut suddenly blazed. Jocelyn had her legs crossed in a way that made her skirt rise higher on her thighs. They were the same luscious thighs he had held on to tightly last night while tasting her.

He tried not to stare. He even tried to stop his body from getting hard, but it was no use. There were some things that a man couldn't control and a physical reaction to a beautiful and sexy woman was one of them. Especially when he happened to be in love with that woman.

He met her gaze, saw the heat in her eyes and saw how she suddenly took her tongue and licked her lips. At that moment all he could think about was taking that tongue, sucking it into his own mouth and having his way with it. He then watched as she switched positions and recrossed her legs, giving him a quick view of her panties. They were white.

He growled low in his throat, not even aware he'd made the sound until a pleased smile touched her lips. "You're trying to tempt me, aren't you?" he asked.

Jocelyn sat back and smiled. "You think so?"

"Yes."

She laughed. "Sounds like you're assuming things, Mr. Steele, and what's your position on people assuming things?"

Positions. Now *that* was something he didn't want to think about at the moment. But then maybe he did...

He slowly crossed the room, not taking his eyes off her, and when he came to a stop in front of where she sat, he reached out for her arm and tugged her unresistingly to her feet, pressing her body to his and gazing deeply into her eyes. "But this time, I'm assuming right."

Jocelyn shivered, feeling the thickness of him pressed against her center. Nice. Hard. Forged of steel. "If you're assuming right, then what are you going to do about it?" she whispered.

His gaze remained locked on hers, and she was struck by passion so intense it was hard for her to swallow. She watched as his eyes darkened. "Don't ask unless you really want to know, Jocelyn."

She sucked in a deep breath when she felt him harden even more against her belly. "I really want to know, and I'm asking," she said, pushing her lower body even closer to his for a more intimate fit.

Now it was Bas who sucked in a deep breath. Bas whose arms wrapped around her tightly. Bas who leaned closer to make sure she saw the desire in his eyes. He moved in closer still and when his mouth was just inches from hers, he snaked out his tongue, slid it sensuously across her lower lip, then the upper one and watched her shudder in response.

"Well, since you really want to know…it's show time," he whispered huskily, before greedily taking her lips with his and picking her up into his arms.

Chapter 14

Bas pulled his mouth from Jocelyn's the moment he placed her on the king-size bed, feeling the insistent throb of desire running rampant all through him.

He hadn't intended to move this fast so soon. He had wanted to give her a chance to get used to him, to accept the place he intended to claim in her life and the intense love he had for her, before they shared ecstasy together. But now fate had stepped in and the need to stamp his claim, brand her as his, was as elemental as breathing. But first, he needed just to hold her, to feel her close to his heart, the heart she now possessed.

"Come here for a second," he said softly, opening his arms to her. And when she slid across the bed to him, into his opened arms, he held her tight, enveloped her into his warmth. She laid her head on his chest, and he knew she could hear the fast beating of his heart, but what she didn't know was that it beat at that pace just for her.

Emotions were churning through him, emotions he'd never before felt for a woman, and now he understood what Chance had meant when he'd said falling in love with Kylie had been like being hit with a ton of bricks. It had happened so fast Chance hadn't been expecting it.

It has been the same for Bas. Love was the last thing he had been looking for when he'd arrived in Newton Grove, but the one thing he'd found with Jocelyn. There was one thing that couldn't be denied with the Steele men. When they found love they knew how to accept it and claim the woman as theirs. At least, it seemed it was that way for three of them. There was no telling how Donovan, who was slow to accept anything at face value and prone to be the most resisting of the four, would handle love once he found it.

Bas's attention was reclaimed when Jocelyn raised her head and smiled at him. Her smile triggered something deep within him. He had to touch her, feel her, taste her all over, have her naked beneath him and join her body intimately with his, make love to her until they were both out of their minds, crazy with need.

And he wanted her now.

He stripped and reached out and began removing her clothes, first her blouse and bra. When her chest was completely bare, the sight of her firm breasts quickened his pulse. He leaned forward, took them in his hands and stroked them, licked them, exhaled hot breath over the hardened dark tips.

And then his hands moved down her waist to remove her skirt while his brain could still function. And when she lay before him in nothing but a pair of white lace panties, he reached out and let his fingertips trace along the edge before touching her moist center. He heard her quick intake of breath, her quiet yet ragged moan. She caught hold of his shoulders as his fingers continued to stroke her with slow caresses. His fingers slipped beneath her panties to touch her intimately, stirring her scent, flaming her heat.

"Bas."

His name was a whispered groan. An earth-shattering moan. And when a purr of pleasure rippled from her throat, he leaned back to pull the scrap of white lace down her legs. Her scent was intense and filled the air surrounding them. A shudder passed through him, the need to mingle in her wet heat became overpowering. But first he wanted to reacquaint his tongue with her taste.

He leaned forward, reached for her hips and lifted her up gently toward his mouth. The moment his tongue entered her she screamed, but he ignored the sound as his tongue continued to push inside her, deep, and then he kissed her intimately, savoring her taste, needing to make love to her in this special and profound way again.

Jocelyn uttered an intense moan while her hips involuntarily rocked against Bas's mouth. No man had ever done this to her before him, and he was making her body crumble into a thousand pieces. She felt every bone in her body melt, and she was filled with intense heat. Her fingernails were digging into his shoulders but she couldn't help it. She was too delirious to do anything but moan in pleasure.

And then he pulled back, cupped her face into his hands and kissed her while easing her back down on the bed, covering her body with his. She felt the ridge of his erection, powerfully aroused, press against the place where his mouth had left its mark, making her thighs tremble. The sensation of his tongue inside her mouth, kissing her deeply, had her moaning incoherently.

When he pulled back she opened her eyes and looked at him, saw the deep-rooted desire in his gaze. She also saw something else in the dark depths, something she couldn't put a name to. "Now I make you mine," he whispered, nudging her legs apart.

With a primal growl he eased inside her while leaning closer and trailing the dampness of his tongue around her earlobe.

Automatically her hips arched and a sizzling groan poured from her lips when he buried himself inside her to the hilt. Their connection, their joining was absolute, complete and so unerringly whole. And at that moment she thought there could not be a more perfect union between two individuals.

"You okay?" he asked, going still to glance down at her.

"Yes," she said while her feminine muscles clamped him, clutched him and claimed him. The sensations she felt were almost more than she could bear. A growing tension, one she didn't understand, begin to stir within her, right there at her center. And as if he knew exactly what she needed, he began to move, rock into her, thrust back and forth, stroke her with a rhythm that made her entire body quiver, fulfilling all her secret desires, her most wanton needs.

Her climax, more intense than any of the others, slammed into her and she screamed his name. She was aware of him driving harder into her, sending her even farther over the edge. She closed her eyes and tightened her muscles around him, milking him and making him groan aloud. She wanted everything she could get from him, determined not to deny herself anything. She wrapped her legs around his waist and locked him in. She had waited too long for this. Too long for a man like him.

"Jocelyn!"

Bas screamed her name while fighting for control. Spasms of ecstasy began tearing through him, and the way her inner muscles were clutching him, draining him, was sending him over into the realms of oblivion. She had stolen his heart and now she was taking over his body, leaving him defenseless and filled with a need he could barely comprehend.

This was love, pure and unadulterated. He had never felt this way before. Nothing had been this intense, invigorating and passionate. And when she let out another scream that split the air, he felt his body explode once again as sensations ripped through him, toppled him over into another world. He lost all sense of everything, except the acceptance that the woman beneath him, to whose body he was intimately joined, was in total possession of his heart, body and soul.

Jocelyn came awake to the sound of Bas's heartbeat. Lying with her head resting on his chest, with his arms wrapped securely around her, and their legs entwined, she felt totally exhausted. But who wouldn't after what they had shared? After making love again in the bed, they had taken the top covers off and moved to a spot in front of the fireplace where they had made love again before falling asleep in each other's arms.

It was still barely light outside and she figured she would have slept right through the night if the growling of her stomach wasn't a reminder that she hadn't eaten anything since lunch.

"Hungry?"

Jocelyn glanced up. Bas was awake and smiling down at her. The flames from the fireplace provided an austere glow to his features. The tone of his voice was sensual and in response to it, she felt a tightening in the lower part of her body. "Yes, I'm hungry," she said, trying to make her voice sound natural.

This was the first time she had awakened in a man's arms after hours of lovemaking. The last time, in college, she had asked the guy to leave her room as soon as it was over, thinking it had been a complete waste of time. But that hadn't been the case with Bas. With him nothing was wasted. They could have been like the Energizer Bunny and kept going and going and going.

"I better feed you or you'll think I'm not a very good host," he said, rising to his feet.

Jocelyn swallowed as she gazed up at him. He was stark naked, unashamedly so. He saw the way she was staring at him and flashed a teasing grin. "If you keep looking at me like that, you might not get dinner after all."

"Then what will I get?" she asked, deciding she might not be as hungry as she'd thought.

"Anything you want. I'm easy."

She moved her gaze lower to a certain part of him. A smile tugged at her lips. "No, you're not. Right now I'd say you're extremely hard."

He chuckled. "You noticed."

"Staring me right in the face, how can I not?"

"Should I apologize?"

She shook her head. "No. What you should do is come back down here and let me take care of it."

He slowly dropped to his knees and then crawled over toward her. "And what do you have in mind?" he asked huskily.

She leaned up and pushed him on his back, then straddled him. "Oh, trust me, Mr. Steele. You're about to find out."

"I can't remember the last time I ate a bowl of chicken noodle soup," Jocelyn said, taking another spoonful into her mouth.

A deep laugh vibrated from within Bas's throat. "Hey, I offered to take you into town to one of those restaurants and you turned me down."

She smiled. "Only because I'm not ready to put my clothes back on. No pun intended but I think we're on a roll."

And that, she thought, was the truth. After making love again in front of the fireplace, they had gotten into the hot tub and made love once more before deciding they needed to eat something to keep their strength up. Bas had let her borrow his robe and together they had gone into the kitchen, where, after checking his empty cabinets, they had found a couple of cans of soup amongst his fishing gear. While the soup had been warming on the stove she had taken the time to call Leah. Her sister hadn't been very talkative, and had, in fact, cut the conversation short, after assuring Jocelyn she was all right.

Satisfied that she had at least spoken to Leah, Jocelyn and Bas had sat down at his kitchen table to enjoy soup and crackers and relish the aftermath of their enjoyment of each other.

Jocelyn figured if she never made love again in her life that would be okay because within the last six hours she had made up for whatever she'd missed in the past and stocked up on what might not be coming her way in the future. But a part of her couldn't imagine sharing anything so intimate with anyone but Bas. Everything the two of them had shared had been utterly amazing. He was definitely a highly charged sexual man.

"Want some more?"

She glanced up at him and smiled. "Some more of what?"

"Jocelyn," he said warningly, "haven't you gotten enough?"

"Of what?" Her tone was innocent. "Soup or you?"

He was sitting across from her at the table wearing just a pair of jeans, and her gaze slid over his bare chest. He was as fine as fine could get and the memories of all those orgasms he'd given her had her body tingling inside out. She wanted to go to him, curl up in his lap, run her hand down his belly, inside his jeans and—

"You're staying all night?"

She moved her gaze back to his face. "Is that an invitation?"

"Yes."

She took another spoonful of soup then asked, "What about clothes?"

"We never did take your luggage out of the car."

"How convenient."

He gave her a knowing look as a smile touched the corners of his mouth. "Yeah, I think so."

Leah finished folding up her laundry and decided that although it was still early she would go upstairs to bed. She heard the doorbell ring and sighed deeply, hoping and praying it wasn't Reese. They had nothing more to say to each other and she wouldn't be able to handle seeing him again that day.

Crossing the room, she wondered who it could be. At the door she asked, "Who is it?"

"Delivery for Leah Mason."

She glanced out the peephole and saw a man of about twenty standing there with a bouquet of flowers in his hands. Still, she had grown cautious over the years. "Do I need to sign for anything?" she asked through the door.

"No, ma'am."

"Please leave whatever you have on the doorstep." She watched as the man did as she requested then walked away. She moved to the window to make sure he got back in his van and drove off. Taking a deep breath, she walked back over to the door and opened it.

She couldn't help but smile upon seeing the beautiful arrangement of calla lilies, her favorite, and knew immediately who'd sent them. Couldn't Reese see what he was trying to do was useless? She would never be the woman that she used to be, a woman who'd enjoyed making love to him anytime and anywhere.

She picked up the bouquet and went back inside the house, locking the door behind her. She placed the arrangement on the table before pulling off the card.

When you hurt, I hurt. Give me a chance to take the pain away. Reese.

Leah continued to read the card, over and over. Why was Reese Singleton so stubborn? Didn't he understand what she'd told him earlier that day? Didn't he get the picture; she was incapable of allowing another man, even him, ever to touch her?

She almost jumped when the doorbell rang again. She went to the door and glanced out of the peephole and her heart began pounding. It was Reese.

A part of her wanted to ignore him, but she knew Reese refused to be ignored. Besides, he evidently hadn't comprehended what she'd been trying to tell him earlier. Maybe if she'd had the help of counselors or a support group earlier than she had, she would be a lot stronger now. But she hadn't. Instead of opening up and talking about it, she had tried to go through life without dealing with the rape, and in so doing she had erected this physical and emotional shield against all men.

Although she already knew the answer, she asked, "Who is it?"

"It's Reese, Leah. Please open the door so we can talk."

Telling him they had nothing to discuss would be useless. It was best to let him in so they could talk and then that would be the end of things.

She slowly opened the door and took a step back and Reese entered, closing the door behind him. She'd seen the look in his eyes the moment he'd gazed at her. The pity she'd expected wasn't there, but what she saw was what she remembered so many

other times—desire. The thought that he still found
her desirable, even after knowing about what Neil
had done, was both flattering and frustrating.

"Why did you come, Reese?"

"Did you think I would stay away?"

No, she really hadn't thought that since he'd
always gone after what he wanted. But she just
couldn't understand why and how he could still love
her after all these years. Especially now.

As if he'd read her thoughts he smiled and said,
"Hey, don't even wonder about it, Leah. You knew
you had my heart from the first."

She couldn't help but release a humorless laugh.
"It was either me or Kristi Alford, and you
deserved better."

He chuckled. "Yes, and you were definitely it. I
have no regrets."

Neither had she. Still, all the good times they'd
shared in the past could not wipe out everything that
had happened.

"Leah, I—"

When he reached out to touch her arm, automatically she pulled back and fear jumped into her eyes
as her entire body went rigid against his touch. She
saw the surprise in his gaze and released a frustrated
sigh. "I told you I get filled with revulsion at the
thought of any man touching me, no matter how
innocent. I think it will be better if you leave now."

He crossed his arms over his chest. "I'm not leaving and I'm not going to let you put distance between us. I understand the barriers you've put up, but I won't let it stop me from proving something."

"Proving what?"

"That to you I'm not a regular guy, Leah. I'm the man you loved and by your own admission, the man you still love. Somehow I'm going to remind you of that and break through those walls you've erected. I'm going to be the one man who'll make you want to be touched again."

She hugged her arms to her breasts and glared at him. "You're pretty sure of yourself, aren't you?"

He smiled. "Yes, and I'm pretty sure of you. You could never resist me when I laid things on thick."

No, she couldn't, but things weren't the same anymore. "But that was then."

"And it could be now if you let it. I want us to get back together. I want to marry you, give you babies we'll both love, and I want to be there for you until the day I die."

The sincerity in his words touched her and she couldn't help the tears that formed in her eyes. Whether he knew it or not, he was offering her a chance to reclaim her dream. But still...

"It won't work, Reese," she said quietly, again trying to make him see reason.

"How do you know if you won't give it a chance? Give us a chance. We can take things slow, start off by going out to eat, to the movies, take walks…and I promise to keep my hands to myself. In fact I will keep my hands to myself until you say you're ready for something more."

She lifted a brow. "No kisses?" She remembered how much they'd liked to kiss.

He smiled softly. "And as much as it will probably drive me crazy, no kisses."

They stared at each other for a long moment and Leah thought about his words, his offer. She met his gaze, studied the expression on his face, looked into the depth of his eyes. "Why do you want to do this? There are other women in town who'd jump at the chance to—"

"You're the one I want, Leah. You're the only one I've ever wanted. You spoiled me for anyone else." He chuckled quietly. "I didn't know just how messed up I was until you left. I haven't been able to get involved with anyone else and it's been a long time."

For him it was a long time, since she knew just how passionate he was. "Why?" she asked.

"Because I couldn't imagine making love to anyone but you."

Leah wondered if he knew what that admission meant to her. But then, if he was putting all his hopes in her, he still might not be making love to anyone. "Reese, I—"

"No. Just say we can make a go of things again, Leah. We'll take thing slow but we'll still make a go. Although we enjoyed the time we were together, for us it was never just about sex anyway. Remember?"

Yes, she did remember. The sex had been good, but they had shared a special friendship, as well. "And you're sure you want to do this?" she asked, needing the reassurance.

"Yes, I'm sure. Let's start off tomorrow. Early. Invite me to breakfast. I miss your pancakes."

She couldn't help the tiny smile that touched her lips. And with the memory she recalled a time when she had prepared pancakes at his place one morning, and how they'd got sidetracked and ended up with more batter over them than in the skillet. Of course they'd had to shower together and she remembered what had happened after that....

Leah blinked. That memory had been totally un-expected. It was the first time she'd been able to recall a man touching her body and not get sick at the thought. And on that particular day Reese had touched her all over.

"So are you going to feed me pancakes in the morning?"

His question reclaimed her thoughts. "Yes, I think I can manage that."

"Good. Well, I'll leave so you can go on to bed and get your rest. See you in the morning, Leah."

After Reese left, Leah felt an inner peace for the first time in a long while.

Chapter 15

Jocelyn gazed down into her coffee before taking a sip and smiled. It didn't seem possible but two weeks had passed since that night she and Bas had spent together and now they were definitely an item. They continued to do a lot of things together. Fun things.

During the day they went their separate ways with him working in the office the majority of the time and with her on the job site. Then, in the afternoons while he was at the gym, she used that time to visit with Leah, at least it had started out that way. But now Reese was dominating a lot of her sister's time and although she knew the two were taking things slowly, just the thought that Leah was spending time with a man, especially the man Leah loved, was gratifying.

Then at night Jocelyn and Bas would meet up somewhere in town, usually at some restaurant or another and enjoy a delicious meal. And since Ms. Sadie had taken Jocelyn into her confidence about Bas's health issues, she made doubly sure whatever he put in his mouth was good for him.

When night came they stayed over either at her place or his. All she had to do was close her eyes to recall any one time his hard male body had entered hers, taking her breath away, preparing her for the orgasm that he could so effortlessly give her, several times over.

At first it was awkward for her, letting a man dominate so much of her time, but pretty soon she got used to him being around. He was considerate, thoughtful and understanding and seemed to know just when she needed her space. He would give it to her, but not for long. It was as if he wanted her to know that what they were sharing was something he intended to make last until the end.

The end.

She knew they were working against a clock and soon he would be leaving to return to Charlotte. She didn't want to think about how her life would be when he left. But she had to be realistic enough to know what they were sharing wasn't forever. He had his life and she had hers. He belonged to the Steele Corporation and she belonged to Mason Construction. Her life was here and his was there. There was no middle ground.

"You're quiet this morning."

Jocelyn glanced up and met Leah's curious stare. "I was just thinking."

"About Bas?" Leah asked, leaning back against the kitchen counter.

Jocelyn opened her mouth to reply, then stopped. She looked closely at her sister. Growing up they had never shared confidences like some sisters who had close relationships. Maybe it was time they did. "Yes, I was thinking about Bas."

"The two of you have been spending a lot of time together."

Jocelyn lifted a brow. "And how do you know that?"

Leah laughed as she poured a cup of coffee. "Hey, give me a break. I wasn't born yesterday. You aren't spending the night here anymore and I doubt you're spending a lot of time at your home in your own bed, so what am I to think?"

After taking a sip of coffee she added, "And don't forget when Reese first became my boyfriend you hadn't even started showing any interest in guys. You much preferred playing the part of the builder and holding on to your virginity."

Jocelyn leaned back in her chair. "Yeah, well, I wish I had held on longer so that Bas could have been my first. I guess in a way he was."

"Yeah, I'm glad Reese was my first as well," Leah said quietly, as she came to the table to sit down.

Jocelyn waited a moment before asking, "And how are things going with you and Reese? I can't help noticing the two of you are spending more and more time together."

Jocelyn watched a tiny smile touch the corners of Leah's lips when she said, "That man is so stubborn." A frown then replaced the smile. "If it was left up to me, we wouldn't be seeing each other at all. It's so unfair to him."

"In what way?"

"Reese is everything a woman could want in a man, and I of all people should know. He's handsome, kind, considerate and understanding. He should be dating someone who can give him the things he needs, instead of someone like me, a woman who can't even think about letting him touch me."

Leah's finger caressed the handle of her cup before she continued. "We've been spending time together for a couple of weeks now and I still can't let him kiss me, although I know he wants to. And he's keeping his word by not asking. He gets here at seven every morning to share breakfast with me and before he leaves I know he's hoping that I'll open up, be responsive and let him, but I can't."

Jocelyn took another sip of her coffee and then said, "At some point you're going to have to try and put behind you that one bad time with Neil and remember all those other great times with Reese." Jocelyn's lips quirked and she added, "I remembered some of your dreams and how you would moan in your sleep. Hell, it made me wish I could have been a fly on the wall during one of those times the two of you were together."

Her comment had Leah laughing and Jocelyn felt good hearing it. When Leah's amusement finally cleared she leaned back in her chair. "Trust me, a fly would have died from too much heat. Reese was all that and then some." A sad smile then touched her lips. "God, I'd love to share some of those times with him again."

"And you can, Leah. Reese is making it possible for you to do that. All you have to do is reach out to him. Don't let what Neil did destroy the most precious thing that mattered to you—your love for Reese Singleton."

A few moments later Jocelyn said, "You know, I use to envy what you had with Reese."

Leah's brows lifted. "You did?"

"Yes."

"Why?"

"Because I knew the two of you were in love, all into each other, and I wasn't there yet with anyone. In fact, I thought the guys who tried talking to me were annoying. I was a daddy's girl who wanted to build things just like he did. I didn't have time for relationships. But that didn't mean I wouldn't occasionally wonder how things could be between a man and woman."

Leah gave her a wry smile. "And I'm sure with Bas you're making up for anything you missed out on."

Jocelyn laughed, thinking of all the things she and Bas had done over the past few weeks; some were outright scandalous, but he had assured her whatever a couple agreed to do in the bedroom was their business. "Yes, you can say that, but what I'm sharing with him isn't forever."

"It can be if you want it. I've seen the two of you together. I think he's quite taken with you. Even Reese mentioned that he was."

Jocelyn shook her head. "Bas is taken with the moment just like I am. We're mature enough to know that one day he's going to pack up and return to that life he has in Charlotte. And I have a lot to do here. This is where I belong, here in Newton Grove, keeping Dad's dream alive."

"And what about your dream? What about love?" Leah asked quietly.

Jocelyn shrugged. "I don't have any dreams and I have no desire to fall in love. I live for the moment. That way you don't worry about what happens when things don't turn out the way you want. And as far as love is concerned, maybe the bug will hit me one day but I'm not in a hurry. What Bas and I are sharing is for today. I'm not planning on any tomorrows."

"And what if he is?"

Jocelyn chuckled. "Trust me, he's not. Bas likes the way things are just as I do."

Leah gazed at her sister a moment before saying, "I think it's all a smoke screen for you, Jocelyn. You do have dreams and you want to fall in love but you're afraid to."

"That's not true."

"I think it is. You missed Mom as much as I did but instead of withdrawing like I did, you turned your attention to Dad and began clinging to him. And then we had Aunt Susan. Now that both Dad and Aunt Susan are gone, you don't want to risk falling in love for fear of eventually losing that person, as well."

Jocelyn stared at her sister for a moment, and then shook her head. She had thought the same thing once and had dismissed the thought entirely from her mind, refusing to find a reason for her lack of interest in falling in love over the years. "I'm not afraid of falling in love or having dreams. I just have more to do with my time than indulging in either."

Leah nodded, and Jocelyn wasn't sure her sister believed what she'd said or not.

Later that night Jocelyn stood at the window staring out. It was dark and cold and according to the news report a little snow might be coming their way. She wouldn't mind the snow, but bad weather wasn't good for a construction company. At least Marcella's house was finished and they had done the closing that day. To everyone's surprise it had gone off without a hitch.

"So this is where you went off to," Bas said, coming behind her and placing a hand around her waist, pulling her back against him. Her turned her into his arms and placed a kiss on her lips. "I missed you."

Jocelyn chuckled. "You didn't even notice me gone, you were so busy painting."

He took her face into his hands. "Trust me I noticed you were gone, but I am enjoying that paint-by-number set. I'm glad you talked me into getting it."

She reached up and slid her arms around his neck. "Umm, paint by numbers today and who knows, you might be asking to use my coloring books tomorrow."

"Not hardly."

She threw her head back and laughed. She and Bas had been having honest-to-goodness fun and she didn't want it to end, but she knew that one day it would. She pushed the thought away, not wanting to dwell on it. "You want to go down in the basement and play a game of pinball?" she asked.

"No, I want you to come back to bed," he whispered huskily against her ear.

Moments later, in bed, Jocelyn wondered how often a woman could come apart in a man's arms. How often could she get filled with so much intense pleasure? The thought of not being able to share this with Bas almost frightened her.

But then Bas leaned over and kissed her, and once again her mind went blank and she let herself drown in the emotions he was making her feel. And when he slid his body over hers, entered her with one long, penetrating sweep, she became totally aware of the size of him as well as his strength.

"That's it. Move with me, baby," he whispered as he began thrusting in and out of her. She moved her hips, clutched him with her thighs, locked him in with her legs and clenched him with her inner muscles, pulling everything she could out of him.

"You're getting it all," he said huskily. The dark sensuality of his voice made her clench him tighter. "Payback."

And the way he paid her back had her moaning out loud. His hands cradled her hips, he pushed deeper inside her, angling her center so he could hit a spot that built pressure near her womb, causing flames to flare to all parts of her loins.

"Bas!"

"Get ready, cause here I come," he whispered hoarsely.

And he came.

His body jerked, bucked, spilled into her, filling her with the essence of him. He threw his head back, breathed in tight before screaming her name. And Jocelyn knew this moment would be engraved in her memory forever.

The next morning Jocelyn was almost too tired and weak to get out of bed, so she decided to stay put just for a little while, and cuddle close to the masculine body that was spooning her naked backside.

She let out a shuddering breath when she thought of last night and all the other nights they had shared.

"You're awake?"

She smiled, wondering if he was asking her that for a particular reason. She turned over and met his drowsy gaze. "Depends on why you want to know."

He wrapped his arms tighter around her. "I need to tell you something."

He sounded serious and she wondered if he was going to tell her that he was leaving. Pretty soon his six weeks would be over and although he claimed he would hang around for at least three months, he really didn't have to. Was he needed back in Charlotte?

"What do you want to tell me?"

"First I need to get my good-morning kiss," he said, leaning over and capturing her lips with his, drinking the essence of her mouth.

When he released her lips, she smiled and said, "Keep that up and we'll never get any talking in."

He slowly pulled back and met her gaze. He reached out and traced his finger along her chin. "I feel things with you that I've never felt before with anyone, Jocelyn, and that can only mean one thing."

She lifted a brow. "What?"

"I love you."

His words, spoken simply, made her think she hadn't heard him right. But then all she had to do was stare into the clarity of his eyes and see both seriousness and sincerity in their dark depths. She felt flooded by emotions she wasn't ready for, and had to swallow a lump that suddenly formed in her throat. "No," she whispered softly. "You can't love me."

Bas reached out and touched his fingertips to her lips. "Yes, I can and you won't believe just how much I do. I want to marry you and—"

Jocelyn pulled away. "Marry me? How can you think such a thing? We can't get married."

Bas's lips tightened in a grim line as he witnessed her reaction to his words. "Yes, we can. Why would you think that we can't?"

Jocelyn pulled herself up in bed. "Because I don't

expect you to move here and surely you don't expect me to just up and move to Charlotte. My life is here. The company is here. This is where I belong, Bas."

"Fine, then I'll move here."

Jocelyn lifted her chin. "And do what? You belong back at the Steele Corporation. Coming here for a while I'm sure was a nice diversion for you but you're going to leave and go back."

Bas blew out a heated breath. "Surely you knew I was falling in love with you, Jocelyn. What do you think these past few weeks have been about?"

"Fun. We were having fun."

"And that's all I've been to you?"

She glared. "I didn't say that, Bas, so don't put words into my mouth. We were indulging in a short-term affair. I'm old enough to know that. I wasn't expecting anything from you, and I most certainly didn't think you were expecting anything of me."

"Well, you assumed wrong."

"And it won't be the first time," she snapped.

The silence between them stretched, and then Jocelyn finally spoke. "Look, it's not that I'm not flattered by your offer because I am. But I can't marry you. My life here is all I know and all I want. Leah was the one who always wanted to leave and move away. I was contented to stay right here. Nothing's changed. That's what I want."

His gaze met hers and the pain she saw there

almost pierced her heart. She hadn't meant to hurt him, but she had. She reached out and touched his arm. "Bas, please understand that—"

"No," he said, pulling away and getting out of bed. "There's nothing left to say. I think you've said it all."

"Breakfast was good as usual, Leah," Reese said pushing the plate away.

She glanced up at him and smiled. "Thanks. I wasn't sure how you would like the mango pancakes. It's a new recipe I tried."

He chuckled. "Hey, I love all pancakes and yours are the best."

She shook her head. "It's a good thing you're as active as you are with how much you consume at breakfast. Going to the gym every day is paying off." And that was true. Reese was in the best shape he'd ever been. The proof was in his jeans. She didn't know of any man who could wear them better or could look sexier in them.

"So what are your plans today?" he asked.

This was how their day started, Leah thought. Reese would arrive for breakfast each morning around seven and she would have everything ready. While he ate a mountain of pancakes and sipped coffee he would tell her his plans for that day and ask about hers. They would then make small talk about the weather, any happenings around town and any other topic of interest. When it was time for him to leave she would walk him to the door and tell him to have a nice day.

When it was time to walk him to the door today, she had just finished telling him about another recipe she planned to try. "Well, don't work too hard today," she said, reaching out to open the door.

"Leah?"

"Yes?" She turned around and met his gaze. He didn't say anything, but then he really didn't have to. Despite years of separation she could still read the look in his eyes.

"Nothing. Don't you work too hard, either," he finally said.

Leah nodded and stood back for him to walk out the door. But some part of her knew she had to make this morning different for them. Jocelyn was right. She couldn't let what Neil had done destroy the one thing that had been so right in her life, the one thing she had cherished the most. Reese's love.

"Reese?"

He turned around. "Yes?"

She didn't say anything at first, then she slowly leaned toward him and, without touching him, brushed a kiss across his lips. She heard his sharp intake of breath and the sound spurred her to go a little further. So she deepened the kiss a little, and when he moaned, she closed her eyes and slipped her tongue inside his mouth.

She got just what she expected and exactly what she wanted, the tantalizing and rich taste of Reese Singleton. This is what time and distance hadn't been able to erase from her memory. Nor had Neil Grunthall.

With excruciating slowness and painstaking thoroughness, she kissed him, leaning into him but careful to keep their bodies from touching. But she needed this. After wondering for years if she'd ever be able to kiss a man again, she had her answer.

Leah slowly pulled back, or at least she tried to, but Reese's mouth followed. He gently leaned toward her, recaptured her mouth, letting her know how much he enjoyed this. So did she. So they kissed again, passionately, thoroughly. And somehow, at some point, he wrapped his arms around her and she didn't reject his touch. She was too caught up in the feel of being in his arms.

Her mind was humming that this was Reese, the man she loved, had always loved and would always love. Finally, he pulled back slightly, then began brushing kisses along her jaw. When he pulled his mouth away, their eyes met and although neither said anything, they were both aware of the importance of what had taken place.

"Thanks for making my day special," Reese said. "It was well worth the wait."

Leah nodded. She then lifted her hands to his chest. "Yes, it was, and please kiss me again."

Reese smiled and lowered his head. He was more than happy to oblige her request.

"The boss is in a bad mood," Tommy Grooms whispered to Reese when he arrived at the work site sometime later. This was their first day on a new project. The post office needed expanding and they had been awarded the job.

Considering he was in a damn good mood, Reese walked over to where Jocelyn was wielding her hammer. He waited until she was finished and tapped on her hard hat. She turned around and glared at him. "What?"

"We need to talk."

Jocelyn mentally swore as she placed her hammer aside and followed Reese into a deserted area of the room. She pulled off her safety glasses and hard hat. "What's this about?"

Reese leaned against a metal post. "You tell me. The guys think you're in a bad mood."

Jocelyn put her safety glasses back on and glared through them. "I am."

"Then you need to leave."

She blinked. "Excuse me?"

"I said you need to leave and pull yourself together. This job is no place for negative emotions right now."

Jocelyn's angered flared. "You're a fine one to talk."

"Yes, and I learned from experience. Go ahead. Take an extended lunch. Come back when you feel better."

"I feel fine."

Reese chuckled without any real amusement. "You might feel fine but you look like hell. It's plain to see you've been crying. What's going on, Jocelyn? You and Bas have a lover's spat?"

She glared. "Don't mention his name."

Reese lifted a brow. "Wow, that sounds deep."

Jocelyn's lips twitched in anger. "Men. All of you are nuts. You want affairs then you don't want affairs. And when you do fall in love, you expect everyone to follow suit like good little soldiers. Well, not everyone wants to fall in love," she snapped.

"Then don't," Reese countered. He then smiled. "But you know what I think, Joce? Whether you want to admit it or not, you're already in love."

Jocelyn decided to have lunch at one of the local sandwich shops in town. Reese had been right. She'd needed time alone. She released a long sigh and thought about what Bas had said that morning. He loved her.

Any other woman would probably have been elated at his confession, but why was she so frightened? She sighed again as the answer came back to her. Mainly because of the unknown. To fall in love with Bas meant uprooting her life here and going someplace outside of her comfort zone. Other than her visits to Aunt Susan every summer in Florida, this was where her life had been. This was where she'd always felt she belonged.

All because of personal insecurities she'd always managed to hide.

Leah was right. The main reason she'd never formed an attachment to a man was because of the fear of eventually being left alone. That was why she'd never been involved in a serious relationship.

Before now. Before Bas.

But he wanted to take her away from here, and as much as she loved him...

Jocelyn's heart began hammering fast and furious in her chest. Reese was right. She was already in love. Suddenly the thought of not being with Bas was something she didn't want to think about and at that moment she knew to deny her love for him was a mistake. She did love him and she had to believe that things would work out and that no matter where he went or where he lived, her place was with him. He was her future as well as her present.

Later that evening Jocelyn knocked on Bas's cabin's door as she went back and forth in her mind what she would say to him. She knew she needed to explain why she had freaked out this morning when he'd told her he loved her, and to make sure that he believed she loved him, as well.

After having lunch she had dropped by to visit Leah, only to find her sister in the best of moods. Leah shared the reason with her. Jocelyn was truly happy for her sister and proud of the progress she'd made with Reese. Now Jocelyn knew she had to get things right with her man, as well.

The door opened and she saw the surprised look on Bas's face. "Jocelyn. I didn't expect to hear from you, especially after this morning."

"I know. May I come in?"

"Sure," he said, stepping aside. She walked in and closed the door behind her.

Bas went to stand in front of the fireplace while Jocelyn remained in the center of the room. "I need to apologize about this morning, Bas."

He held her gaze. "Evidently I hit a sore spot."

Jocelyn nodded. "Yes, the thought of ever loving anyone has been a personal insecurity I've refused to acknowledge. For some reason I've equated falling with love with eventually losing that person. So, to play it safe, I never allowed myself the luxury of truly loving anyone. Until you."

He raised to his lips the glass he was holding in his hand and took a sip, never letting his eyes stray from hers. "And do you? Do you love me, Jocelyn?"

She smiled, hoping he would see the truth in her eyes. "Yes, I love you, Bas. Reese sent me away from the job site this morning so I could go someplace and rationalize things, and I did. I can't let life pass me by without having dreams, and without having love. I love you, Bas, and if your offer still stands, I want to be your wife."

Bas set his drink on the mantel and came to stand in front of Jocelyn. "The offer still stands, sweetheart," he said in a husky voice, reaching out and cradling her face in his hands.

"There's one thing you're going to discover about a Steele, Jocelyn. When we find the woman we want, that's it. We don't give up until we have her. I heard what you said this morning but there was no way I was going to give you up without a fight. What I have to offer you is my love for the rest of your days, Jocelyn. I believe in my heart there was a reason your father wanted me here and now I know what that reason is. You. All I'm asking is that you trust me enough to know that I love you, I'll take care of you and keep you safe for the rest of my life. And I meant what I said. I don't have to return to Charlotte. I'll be content living right in this town with you, as long as the two of us are together."

Tears sprang into Jocelyn's eyes. This beautiful man was willing to make sacrifices for her. "No, everything is worked out now. I've talked to Reese and

Leah. They've agreed with my decision to sell the company to Cameron Cody, granted he agrees to all of the concessions I want him to make. That way Reese can use the money Dad left him to start his own business. Leah plans to stay and if things continue to work out, she will eventually open a restaurant next to Reese's shop."

She then smiled brightly. "It seems that Reese and Leah are making progress, so I'll be selling Reese back their home. That means I won't have a place to live. Any ideas?"

Bas took a step closer to her. "Baby, I have plenty. But are you sure you want to sell the company? I know how much Mason Construction means to you."

"Yes, but it was Dad's dream and not really mine. My dream is to be with you, Bas. To love you, marry you and start a family with you. I want lots of babies."

Bas laughed and pulled her into his arms. He held her for a moment before pulling back slightly and capturing her lips with his. The kiss seemed to last forever. When it ended, he pulled her closer into his arms and whispered against her hair, "You want lots of babies, do you?"

Jocelyn chuckled. "Yes, plenty of Steeles."

Bas swept her into his arms and headed for the bedroom. "That's good because I'm ready to give you everything you want, sweetheart."

Epilogue

"I like her, Bas."

Bas smiled at Chance over the rim of his wine-glass. "Glad you do because I happen to love her."

Chance chuckled. "That doesn't surprise me."

"I figured it wouldn't."

Chance took a sip of his own drink before asking, "So, have you asked her yet?"

Bas's smile widened. "Yes, and she's said yes. We're planning to wed before the end of the year. That will give her time to wrap up a few things she has going on in Newton Grove, which includes selling the construction company to Cameron."

Chance nodded. "When are you going to tell the family?"

"Later tonight after the party."

"I wish you all the best."

"Thanks and every time I look over at Jocelyn, I know that she is just that. The best."

Later that night, after Donovan's birthday party, Jocelyn snuggled closer in Bas's arms thinking how her day had gone. She had fallen in love with his family the moment she'd met them all, his brothers, cousins and parents.

Chance's wife, Kylie, was simply too nice for words, and Kylie's best friend, a Queen Latifah look-alike named Lena Spears, was also kind. Jocelyn smiled when she thought about his female cousins, Vanessa, Taylor and Cheyenne. There hadn't been a dull moment with the three of them around.

Jocelyn had noticed the heated looks Cameron Cody had given Vanessa all evening, and the same held true for the looks Morgan Steele had given Lena.

"So what do you think, Bas? Which couple will it be?"

Bas pulled her closer into his arms. He knew what she was asking since she had shared her observations with him earlier. "It will be awhile for Cameron. Vanessa is a hard one to thaw so he has his work cut out for him. My brothers and I are hoping it will be Morgan and Lena. The more she resists him, the moodier he gets. But like I told you, a Steele eventually gets what he or she wants."

Jocelyn lifted her head and gazed down at him. Her expression was suddenly serious. "And did you get what you wanted, Bas?"

He pulled her back down to him, wrapped his arms around her. "I got everything I wanted and more, Jocelyn. I love you."

"And I love you."

And when their mouths connected they knew that they were once again about to generate a little night heat.

Leila Owens didn't know
how to love herself let alone
an abandoned baby
but Garret Grayson knew
how to love them both.

She's My Baby

Adrianne Byrd

(Kimani Romance #10)

AVAILABLE SEPTEMBER 2006

FROM KIMANI™ ROMANCE

Love's Ultimate Destination

Available at your favorite retail outlet.